THE ORC BLACKSMITH'S BRIDE

ORC OUTCASTS
BOOK 2

K.L. WYATT

Copyright © 2024 by Kayla

All rights reserved.

No part of this book may be reproduced in any form or by any electronic or mechanical means, including information storage and retrieval systems, without written permission from the author, except for the use of brief quotations in a book review.

Contact: authorklwyatt@gmail.com

Cover Art by: Impyeu

E-book ISBN: 978-1-963211-03-0

Paperback ISBN: 978-1-963211-04-7

CONTENT WARNING PAGE

For content warnings please scan here:

DEDICATION

To anyone who has ever been fucked over by a man, your happily ever after is right around the corner.

PREFACE: IVY

As I sprint towards the swamp's edge, my slippers dig into the muddy ground. My heart is racing so fast it feels as though it's going to beat out of my chest. Excitement and nerves mingle into one. Tonight is the night I will run away with my beloved Sorin, and he will finally make me his bride.

I pause briefly to take in my surroundings. The sun had set not too long ago, and now, the full moon beams in the night sky. I embrace the cool breeze that tickles my cheeks and continue toward our meetup point. I waited longer than expected to exit from my crumbling cabin to ensure that I didn't run into my Uncle Edmund. He's usually home from the tavern by now and passed out on the floor. A seed of doubt creeps into my mind, but I'm already running out of time. I need to leave now or risk Sorin thinking I abandoned him. No, that wouldn't do. My uncle is probably passed out at the home. I have no reason to worry about running into him. He has spent most of his days drinking ever since his brother, my father, died.

My chest tightens at the memory of my father. He was my world until he was murdered when I was twelve. My uncle and he were as thick as thieves, and when money got tight, it was a no-brainer for them to join a local militia group. It wasn't a glamorous job; in fact, I think they saw a lot of horrors, but my father and uncle were skilled swordsmen, and it paid well. One day, he and my uncle left, promising to be back for supper, but only Uncle Edmund returned.

"Your father is dead." His words replay in my head over and over again. He said it with so much coldness. His icy stare bored into my soul as he looked upon my face, which must have reminded him of his brother. From that moment on, Uncle Edmund nurses liquor bottles to escape his reality. The reality in which he had to live in a world without his best friend.

However, "living" is too strong of a word to describe my uncle for the past eight years. Sure, he still breathes, but his mind died along with my father. I have a lot of empathy for my uncle, even though that empathy isn't reciprocated. My uncle's resentment is not lost on me.

But I'm eighteen now, and I don't want to live in a hole of grief any longer. After tonight, I will be far away from this village, living with the love of my life.

Sorin arrived in our small village over a month ago, and while he is a few years older than me, I still caught his special attention. For the life of me, I couldn't understand why. So many other amiable girls in our town are far better off than me. I have no dowry. My uncle's only income is pawning off my father's old things, and the little coin he makes from that is spent all on booze.

But Sorin doesn't care about the material things in life. No, he sees me for who I truly am. He says I am smart, beautiful, and funny. As is he, which is why I love him so much. He spent weeks being a complete gentleman courting me until he finally proposed we run away together under the most beautiful pine tree. I couldn't contain my love for him and gave myself to him in my entirety.

I blush, thinking of the memory of his hand caressing my hips and his cock sliding into my virgin sheath. He declared that I was the love of his life and that he would rather die than be with anyone else. All I had to do was scrounge some money for our great escape. I, of course, knew that our departure wouldn't be free, not to mention *scandalous*. But as long as Sorin married me, everyone would be none the wiser that I had given him my virginity before the wedding. My reputation will stay intact as long as we leave tonight. So, for the past week, I've been stealing coins from my Uncle Edmund's coin purse when he was passed out drunk on our floor.

Earlier this morning, I received a note from Sorin, stating I should leave the pouch of the coin under the tree where we first made love and meet him at the swamp's edge when the sun goes down. When he first suggested we travel through the swamplands, I protested. Everyone knows you stay far away from that treacherous place unless you are a brave tradesman. Only the most desperate seek to trade with the vicious creatures of the swamp. The most notorious, Orcs. But Sorin reassured me that all would be well. After a bit of arguing, I finally conceded.

I finally reach my destination, which Sorin mapped out, and wait anxiously. I grasp the hood that cloaks my identity. If there are any tradesmen around these parts, I don't want to take the chance of any of them getting a good look at my face and telling people back in the village. News travels quickly in our town, and a young girl near the swamp's edge would spread like wildfire. I don't want to risk my uncle finding us out before we put ample distance between us.

Time passes, and I bite my lip in anticipation; surely,

Sorin should be arriving soon. But then my mind wanders to darker places. What if he was caught?

A nearby rustling bush dashes any fear from the mind.

"Sorin! I was so scared you—" My words stop short as the man in front of me reveals himself not as Sorin but as my uncle Edmund.

"You foolish girl," he growls.

"Uncle Edmund, w-what are you doing here?" I stumble over my words.

"Trying to save you from this fucking mess you created."

"What?" I take a few apprehensive steps back.

"Don't tell me you actually believed that treacherous worm," he spits. "What am I saying? Of course, you did. That's why this is happening."

"Uncle Edmund, I don't under—"

"He is a con artist," he cuts me off. "Sorin probably isn't even his real name. I've met plenty of his type when your father and I were on the road. They go town to town, convincing young maidens to give them their coin in exchange for marriage."

"No, Sorin wouldn't do that!" I shake my head in disbelief. It can't be true. I start recounting every interaction that Sorin and I ever had.

"Believe it, sweetheart. You got duped." Uncle

Edmund's breath still reeks of ale. "I knew my coin purse felt lighter. I had thought some of the boys at the bar were swiping some off of me. I hadn't figured you were foolish enough to fall for something like this until I overheard whispers in town."

"The whispers?" I squeak, afraid of what he is going to say next.

"Word on the street is that you are no longer a virgin. Completely sullied and undesirable." He looks at me with disgust.

"We were going to get married!" I cry out.

"He was never going to marry you!" he screams and grabs my shoulders as tears cascade down my cheeks.

"You fucked him like a no-good whore, and I'm going to be stuck with you my whole miserable life." He growls so close to my face that I shut my eyes tightly. Uncle Edmund has always been cruel, but I've never been as scared of him as I am now. I wriggle my way out of his grasp, and without thinking, I grab a dagger out of my boot. Before my father passed away, he spent his free time teaching me swordsmanship. I hated it, but he always reminded me that people in this world may want to hurt me. Little did he know it would be his own brother.

"Uncle Edmund, this isn't my fault!" I sob, pointing

my small dagger at him, trying to get him to desperately understand.

A humorless laugh escapes his lips, which is all the more threatening than his rage.

"Everything is your fault. Your father and I only worked that job so he could afford to buy you that stupid straw doll you wanted. He is dead because of *you!*" His words slap me across the face and sting more than Sorin's registering betrayal.

"No...no!" I attempt to catch my ragged breath, and while I try to remember the basic sword training my father gave me, Uncle Edmund disarms me swiftly by barging into my body.

THUD. I shriek as I fall to the ground. My hands skid across the cold ground, and my dress tears. I welcome the pain as I lay face down in the dirt, sobbing uncontrollably. Sorin's gentle touches, mingled moans, and gentle praises were all lies. He is truly not coming, and I, with everyone knowing I am no longer a virgin, am ruined. Not only that, but now I know the true reason for my uncle's ire. If I was him, I would hate me too. I swear I can feel my heart burst into a million little pieces. My uncle is right, I am a fool.

Pulling out a flask from his tattered coat, Uncle Edmund hovers over me as he brings the old metal to his lips. Taking a swig seems to relieve some of his anger.

"The only reason I didn't cast you out was because I promised him before he died that I would take care of you. But I'll never love you, and I will never forgive you." His voice is laced with contempt. A few heartbeats pass, and my ragged cries are the only response I can muster. Uncle Edmund crouches down next to my soiled body and simply states, "I wonder what your father would say if he found out his daughter grew up to be a whore," before walking off like he didn't just deliver the fatal blow to my heart.

I lay face down on the muddy ground for the entirety of the night, praying to the gods that something in the forsaken swamp would devour me whole. Unfortunately for me, my prayers were never answered.

1

EVRIN

Four years later...

F I rub my hand over my face in a feeble attempt to banish my exhaustion. I've been so tired ever since I spoke to Kal. He is our clan's animal trapper and was a fellow outcast who ended up catching a human female in one of his traps. The latest news is that she just gave birth to twin girls. I can't help the deep-seated jealousy brewing under my thick skin. Around a hundred years ago, the female orc population started to decline. The elders desperately searched for answers but found none. Since then, it was agreed that orc males would be an outcast from the clan when they came of age and could only return if they found a female to breed and wed. Normally, this would be another orc female, but since Kal's human wife gave birth to girls, our mating pool has widened. I want nothing more than to have a wife and kits, but I fear Kal's situation was merely a stroke of luck. How will I ever find a human mate if they are forbidden to enter the swamp we call home?

I try my best to expel the thoughts that have eaten away at me for the past few months. I must focus on the task at hand: meeting at the rendezvous point on the edge of the swamplands with one of my regular tradesmen. Orcs and humans don't typically trade with each other, but very little iron can be found in the swamps. As a blacksmith, that poses quite an issue. Normally, our swamp clan trades with an orc clan in the mountains. But since news of a wedded and bred human reached them, they have cut off all communications. They are foolish orcs who believe the species should remain "pure." Gah! They have lost their minds. What a blessing it is to have a mate. Why anyone would reject such a bond for the simple sake of purity is beyond me.

But their lack of cooperation has forced me to work with the humans. Something I had hopes in which I could meet a female mate but was sorely disappointed to discover every human tradesman is a male who doesn't have the guts to meet an orc face to face. Instead, we operate solely on a drop-and-collect basis. The only reason I know they are all males is because, for the first month, I watched them from afar. They are blissfully unaware of a predator that lurks in the distance. I must say that humans have terrible survival instincts.

Just as I reach my collection point, I hear rustling in nearby bushes. I reach for one of the swords strapped to my back and ready myself. We might just be outside the swamplands, but that doesn't stop some creatures. I round a tree, and my body stills. It is no creature.

It is a human female.

I quickly return my blade to my back and gape at her in stunned silence.

Her back faces me as she is crouched down, carefully picking berries and filling her woven basket. She has bright fire-colored hair, pale skin, and an ample bosom. My cock immediately stiffens at the sight of her. What is she doing this close to the swamplands? I'm overjoyed by her presence, but my immediate reaction is to protect her from the unknown dangers of the swamp. My question is quickly answered as I observe the small blue fruit in between her delicate fingers. They are swamp berries. They are delectable sweet fruits, but humans are generally unfamiliar with them. Understandable, as they only grow in the swamp or near the swamplands.

I've never seen a human female before, and I swear I forget how to breathe momentarily. Everything about her is perfect: her thick thighs, her wide hips, and rosy red cheeks.

I've always been an orc of action, at least until now. I, of course, want to rut her into the ground, but I also want to observe her. Get to know her. What does her voice sound like when she is moaning my name? What will she make with those berries? Does she taste as sweet as she looks? I have a million questions, but I am not brave enough to ask one. So, instead, I watch her.

She completes her work and is content with the now full basket of berries. None the wiser, this human female has no idea that an orc stalks her from a distance. My anxiety piques at her lack of spatial awareness. Many dangers lurk in this world, waiting to strike against someone as delectable as her. I desire nothing more than to drag her back to my cabin, where I can keep her safe.

I follow her down a dirt path, close enough to keep her in my line of vision but not close enough to alert her to my presence. I've never ventured this far into the human lands before, but I'm entranced by this seductress. The hem of her dress drags along the road, dirtying it, but she doesn't seem to mind. By the looks of her blue tattered gown, she is used to working in this attire. Odd, why don't human females wear something more practical?

It doesn't take long until she arrives at a decaying cabin. Surely, this can't be where she lives. There appear to be no other human homes in sight. Where is her clan? Is she an outcast like me?

She stops in front of the door, and it creaks open. It is practically hanging off of its hinges. I get a glance at her face before she enters her home, and although it's stunning, there is a hint of sadness to it.

I'm completely enthralled by this woman, and the second I lose sight of her, I am desperate for more. I survey our surroundings and deem a nearby hill to be my best vantage point. I use bushes and trees to hide my presence and dance along the property line until I reach my spot.

"I guess I'm not completely useless," I whisper to myself and crouch into the position that looks directly into two windows. I gaze into what appears to be a poorly lit bedroom and a common room. Up until this point, it is like I have lost every skill I've learned over the last twenty-six years.

I see something move in the common room window and my body stills. I register the presence of a male. I already feel incredibly possessive over this female, and having another male nearby will turn ugly fast. I let out a growl. The second I laid eyes on her near the swamp I knew that will be my bride and the mother of my kits.

Before I grab one of the swords strapped to my back, the human male stumbles into a better view. I watch as he brings a metal container to his lips and sways around. The man is drunk and...way too old to be the human female's mate. This must be her father, then. I breathe a sigh of relief, although I'm still not happy he is in her presence. My sweet human doesn't seem to enjoy his company either; she looks upon him with apathy, not love.

What has happened to this poor creature to make her so sullen with her own loved ones? I would give nothing more than to have my parents back.

She places the basket of swamp berries on a table and saunters into the dark bedroom. I grunt in frustration. I can't see a thing, and my cock is begging to get a glimpse of her beautiful round figure.

Time passes, and I grow agitated with every moment. I double-check that her father stays in the common room; I would have no qualm killing him if he dared stumble into her room. Candlelight starts flickering as my human ignites them one by one. It takes my orc eyes time to adjust to the sudden change in brightness. I see pieces of her bright hair flicker into view and flashes of pale, freckled skin. Gah! This godsforsaken window is too small!

But just as my frustration piques, my vision adjusts,

and I see a floor-length mirror positioned perfectly for my viewing pleasure. She finally meanders in front of the mirror, and I have the best fucking angle of her fat ass and large breasts. She is wearing a white corset, some frilly white shorts, and stockings that taunt me. Her outfit hugs each and every one of her voluptuous curves in all the right places. By the gods, I nearly come just at the sight of her. But something in the back of my mind starts to eat away at me. Why does her appearance unnerve me? My human looks at herself in the mirror, appreciating her hand-sculpted body from the gods, and it suddenly dawns on me.

Humans wear all white to their weddings.

I feel my face pale, and rages boil my veins. No, she will not be someother's bride. She is *mine!*

I take no time to think through my actions before I sprint down the short hill. I will not take any chances that this human weds another. For a split second, I debate, entering through the window. But I quickly realize I won't fit. The only opportunity to enter the cabin will be through the front door.

Without hesitation, I round the corner of the house and kick down the rotting door. I do not attempt subtly; this weak male and my sweet human are the only humans around.

"What the fuck—" the man screams and falls onto

his ass. Maybe seeing an orc in his unkempt home will sober him up.

"Uncle Edmund?" My redheaded human opens the door to the bedroom but screams when she registers my presence. Ah, he is her uncle, not her father.

"Ivy!" the human named Edmund shrieks.

"Ivy..." I play with her name on my tongue. Gorgeous, just like her.

I charge past Ivy's uncle as he struggles to his feet and barge through the bedroom door that she attempts to slam close. Ivy has both weight and height, but her strength is no match to mine.

"What do you want, you beast!" she yells.

I wince at her words. I want this sweet human to welcome me into her arms and body. At the moment, she is doing neither.

"You," I growl; I can't help my aggression. The idea of another male marrying my bride has me frayed at the edges.

"Me?" she whispers, confused.

A sudden jolt of laughter sounds from the common room. Her uncle laughs hysterically, "You want...Ivy? You can have her!"

Although he offers me what I desire the most, I can't help but grind my teeth together. I look back towards Ivy, and her expression tells me enough. She stares at me like wild prey who knows they are about to be eaten. Her wide-eyed expression and rapid breaths show both her fear and her sadness.

"You would give up your own niece to a beast?" I ask with my voice laced with disgust. I know I will give Ivy the best life. She will be loved, protected, and cared for by me. But this coward of a man doesn't know that.

"That whore? I've been trying to get rid of her for the past four years!"

"What did you call her?" I pull a sword from the back of my sheath and charge the drunk bastard. Ivy yells something, but I can't hear her. My ears ring, and my eyes blur with rage. Edmund, now on his feet, has found a blade of his own and does his best to match my strikes. It is clear he has had decent training yet he stands no chance against me. I block his every advance until I finally land a punch to his stomach. Edmund slouches over, and I take my opportunity to disarm him by slicing my blade through his right wrist. He won't ever pick up a blade again.

"Fuck!!" he screams in pain. "My hand!"

"Don't worry, your head will soon be joining it," I grit out and raise my blade again to deliver the fatal blow.

"Don't kill him! Please!" Ivy begs as she runs towards me. My anger dims almost immediately, and I shift my focus to her.

"Please don't kill him! I will go with you," she begs. "I promise, but just don't kill him. I've killed enough people in my family."

I don't understand what she is referring to, yet I can't deny my beautiful bride anything.

"But he disrespected you. It is an offense that can only be remedied with a battle to the death. I am protecting your honor," I try to explain myself. She will soon come to learn orc traditions.

"Honor? I don't have much of that these days," she murmurs.

"My fucking hand!" Edmund cries, cradling his bleeding stub.

I look down at the pathetic creature but ultimately succumb to my wife-to-be's wishes. Why she desires to keep her uncle alive after how he treats her is beyond me. I lower my blade and hear her sigh of relief. But not me. No, I have no form of relief. I'm currently a giant mass of tension. My anger and lust have reached a boiling point.

It is time to return to the swamp.

I slide my sword back into the sheath strapped to my back.

"Thank you—" she starts, but I cut her off by wrapping my arm around her ass and throwing her over my shoulder.

"HEY! Put me down!" Ivy shrieks.

Within a few strides we are exiting the small crumbling cabin with only her uncle's soft sobs lingering in the distance. Ivy beats on my back, calling me names, but I pay her no mind. I finally have a bride. It might take her time to accept me. But soon enough I will have a wife full of my seed and a pussy that is all mine. I will no longer be an outcast.

2

IVY

It doesn't take long before we are deep into the swamp. Forbidden lands to my people but home to the orcs. My head is still spinning with the events of the evening, but I decide to focus my thoughts on my current predicament, hanging over the shoulder of my captor. When the beast first slung me over his back, I spent all my energy kicking and screaming until I completely exhausted myself. I quickly realized that any attempt to escape him while I was in his arms was futile. So, instead, I resigned myself to tracing the sharp lines of his muscles without making contact with his skin.

Despite his firm grasp around my waist and being in nothing but my undergarments, I determined that brushing my fingertips across his back would feel too intimate. Alternatively, I opted to use my imagination.

Luckily, I didn't have to use much of it. The male only wears trousers and a few leather straps across his chest to sheath his swords. Everything else was exposed green skin. That lasted until the darkness enveloped us. Now, I am left with nothing but frantic thoughts swimming through my mind.

I shake my head, trying to distribute the blood that has concentrated on my skull. I shift uncomfortably, which only causes the creature to tighten his grip.

I roll my eyes. Like I could possibly get away. I had already tried that and quickly learned how pointless it was. I even thought about grabbing one of the swords strapped to his back. I knew I could wield it, just not from this position. The blades were not a standard length for humans; no, these were approximately double the size. I couldn't even remove them from their sheath at my current angle.

For reasons I still don't understand, this beast has no intention of letting me go. And to my dismay, I have no choice but to accept it for now.

"*You.*" His guttural voice repeats in my head over and over again. The way he said it, with such possessiveness, scared me in more ways than one. What could this creature possibly want from me? He hasn't muttered a word since he slung me over his shoulder. And for fuck's sake, I don't even know his name. My uncomfortable thoughts make me squirm again, and he grunts his disapproval.

I freeze in response. Did he really just grunt at me? I try my best to let out a controlled, steady exhale, but this beast is testing my nerves. I've accepted being his captive. I have accepted being carried around like a sack of grain, by the gods. By the gods, I even accepted my lack of dignity. But what I won't accept is disrespect. One moment, I was picking sweet berries, and then the next, I was stolen from my home by the very beasts I'd only ever heard about in stories. The least he could do was speak to me.

"Put me down now!" I grit out every word. I'm tired, hungry, and, more than anything, sick of being scared.

"Do you hear me, foul beast? I said put me down now!" I pitch my voice, beating my fist against his back. He probably won't let me go, but that doesn't mean I can't make it increasingly uncomfortable for him. I will wield whatever power remains. And right now, that means being the most annoying human he has ever met. A thought passes my mind: Has he even met any other humans?

"I can barely feel my arms! Now put me do—" I yelp as I'm suddenly thrust back over his shoulder and onto the wet mossy ground. The world won't stop spinning. I don't even attempt to stand as I know I will simply fall back on my ass. Although I can't see anything, I feel the beast's presence approach and loom over me. Without looking up at him, I can sense his predator's gaze. My skin prickles at the sensation. I fear him, yet there's something else I can't describe. I exhale steadily, but this time to calm my nerves, not my frustration.

"Welcome home," the male mutters. "You want to walk? Walk."

He grabs me by my arm with a commanding grip that pulls me to my shoeless feet. I let out a little squeak as I feel the moisture from the ground seep into my black stockings. The sensation makes my skin crawl and provides a momentary distraction from his words. Did he just say...home? This is it? But there are no other orcs. Maybe there are, and I just can't see them.

Even in the dark, I wasn't prepared for how utterly exposed I feel. My legs wobble underneath me. I don't know how long we have been traveling, but it was long enough for my legs to lose sensation. Without thinking, I grab onto the orc's strong forearms to steady myself. He makes a low groan that could be interpreted as pain, but that wouldn't make sense. Surely, my hands could not affect this creature's thick skin.

"Fine," I bite out. I want him to know that I will walk on my own, not because he told me to. I push off of his arm and start walking. I use my hands and small steps to guide me in the pitch black. The male behind me places a gentle hand on my back, and my spine goes rigid in response. His touch...unnerves me. I wouldn't expect something his size to be so tender.

My hands finally brace something, which I realize is some kind of railing. Soon after, my feet hit a platform, which could mean only one thing...stairs.

I swallow my humorless laugh. The orc didn't release me because I demanded it. He did it simply because we reached his lair or whatever the fuck this is. What is his aim now? To watch me struggle up these stairs? To embarrass me? I've been embarrassed enough for a lifetime.

I pause briefly, and I can feel him rustle behind me. I weigh my options; I can either attempt to do this on my own or ask him to carry me...

Fuck both options. I'm not doing either.

I plop back to the ground in defiance. Sure, it's childish, but it's the only move I have.

"Move, female," the orc grunts out. He sounds almost tired. Perhaps his patience is also running thin.

That makes two of us.

Instead of responding, I simply clamp my mouth shut. Maybe if I pretend like I didn't exist, I will be left alone. One can only hope.

"Female!" The beast reaches down to pull me

upright, but I let my body go completely slack. He howls out his frustration. "You infuriating creature! I've had enough of this." And with those words, I am once again scooped up in his arms. So much for making it difficult for him.

I cross my arms against my chest and do my best to avoid eye contact, which is easier said than done. It's like the darkness enveloped everything but his amber eyes.

Before I know it, we have ascended the staircase. He kicks down the door, and a small lit candle in the corner of the cabin illuminates the small space. It takes a few moments for them to adjust, but soon, I make out the countless blades that cover the entirety of the walls. They're...breathtaking. Did he make all of these? They distract me from the simplicity of the room. Aside from the blades, there's only a decently sized straw bed, no doubt to accommodate his size, a table, and a singular chair. It seems like he doesn't entertain much.

However, the moment of observation is short-lived as he steps towards the bed, reaching it in only a few strides. Fear spikes in my chest. Despite what townspeople think of me, I am not knowledgeable in the way of sex. I can't—I *won't* do this with him. Before my panic can find its way to the surface, the beast simply tosses me onto the crunchy bed.

"Hey!" I shout accusingly.

"That's what you get for acting like a child," he scolds.

"Me?" I gape at him, completely dumbfounded by his words. I can finally make out his face under the candlelight. I swear my heart skips a beat, so I rub the space below my clavicle. Indeed, this is caused by the anxiety of everything I have endured today and not by this creature's appearance. His features are sharp yet uncharacteristically handsome. Because of his height, I have to crane my neck upwards to get a good look at him. He doesn't shrink under my observation; instead, he holds firm. If he intends to intimidate me, it's working. He isn't lean in the slightest, and his muscles bulge, making him the most heavily built male I have ever seen.

"You cannot be seriously scolding me after you just broke into my home and whisked me away against my will. Not to mention, you assaulted my uncle. Thanks to you, he is without one hand."

"Your uncle," he growls, "should be happy he still has his head."

I let out a humorless laugh. This conversation is utterly ridiculous. "What is it that you want with me?" I ask flatly.

"To be my bride," he answers plainly.

My blood runs cold. No. Surely not. Without thinking, I grab one of the blades from the wall and assume the fighting stance my father taught me all those years ago. To my surprise, the orc doesn't even flinch, but I don't let his dismissive glare deter me. People have been underestimating me my whole life. My father always said to use people's misplaced perceptions of you against them. So, I harden my resolve to fight the beast for my life.

"That is impossible. I'm not suitable for marriage. Did someone pay you for this? Did my uncle pay for this? To steal me away as some cruel joke. What? I'm so undesirable that only an orc would marry me."

I don't miss him flinching at my last sentence, but instead of reacting in anger, he simply lets out a sigh of exasperation.

"You don't belong to your uncle or any other male. No one paid me. No one bribed me. And no one forced me. They wouldn't dare, for it would mean their death. You are mine simply because I wished it."

I fiddle with the sword's grip, and I can tell he notices. My heart skips a beat, and I immediately know it will cost me. The sword's hilt weighs heavy in my hand. I didn't exactly have time to pick out one that fit me, now did I?

The best bet I have is to go in for the attack, so that's exactly what I do. The creature counters me with little to no effort, pinning my arms and stealing the blade. I scream out in frustration and grit my teeth at him. But as he looks down at me, I swear a faint smile dances across his lips.

"I'm not someone you want to marry," I whisper.

"Why? Because you intended to marry someone else. That is why you wear all white, isn't it? I don't care who the male is; you are mine and the only one I want to marry." He stares so deeply into my eyes that I feel like he sees my soul stripped naked. It scares me completely, and his words make me want to cry. Why is he doing this to me?

"I-I," I stumble on my words, not knowing which one of his words to address. The preposterous notion that anyone would want to marry me or that I would ever be caught dead being married in my undergarments. I decide to comment on the latter.

"This isn't a wedding dress! These are my...well... they are my underwear." I look towards the ground, embarrassed to look at him as I continue, "Besides, no one would want to marry me. You included. I do not have my virtue. You see...I'm not a virgin. I'm spoiled goods." The admission is still painful to admit, even to this creature.

I brace myself to look at his horrified expression, but what I see is only confusion. He looks at me with an inquisitive brow, like what I said meant nothing to him.

Now, it's my turn to stare at him with confusion. He has to care. *Everyone* cares about a woman's virtue. My people have practically shunned my uncle and I since the rumor spread that I no longer have my maidenhood.

"I, too, am no virgin." He pauses, leans towards me, causing me to squirm, and takes a deep whiff. "And you do not smell spoiled to me."

"But you are a—" I stop myself before saying the word *man* to describe the being before me. Because he is no man.

"You don't care that I am not a virgin?"

"Why the fuck would I care about that?" His voice carries a tinge of irritation like he doesn't understand why this is even a discussion. Now, his proposition scares me even more. The orc, whom I still don't know the name of and who intends on marrying me, pulls me close into his embrace, and for the first time, I feel the outline of his angry boner. My breath catches in my throat as he whispers, "Listen to me and listen to me closely. I don't care who claimed your heart before; your pussy is mine."

Despite my better judgment, my core tightens. I squeeze my eyes shut, trying to get a handle on the situation and my spiraling feelings. He pulls back, and without his presence, I feel like I'm going to fall. I grab onto the bedpost as he makes his way to the door.

"Get some rest. In the morning, we will leave for The Chosen One."

"The chosen what?" I try to make sense of his words.

"The Chosen One. It is a tree deep in the swamp. It's where my people go to complete a marriage and their mating bond. Tonight will be your only chance to get a full night's sleep before I fill each and every one of your holes with my seed."

He pauses for a response, but I have lost the ability to form words. I notice the subtle clench of his jaw before he opens the door to leave.

"Wait!" I stumble towards him, and he slowly turns from the door.

"W-what is your name?" I whisper.

"Evrin."

Silence fills the room before I remind myself of my manners. Although everything that has transpired between us states that we are well past formalities, manners are the only thing I can control now. I simply respond, "My name is Ivy."

"I know." And before I know it he has left the cabin, closing the door behind him.

I should welcome the distance, but his lack of presence makes our interactions sink deeper. It's like his very being is seeping into my bones. Perhaps the shock is wearing off, but a sudden wave of despair washes over me. I hug my waist, willing myself not to cry. I haven't felt this alone since that dreadful night four years ago.

CLINK CLINK CLINK.

The rhythmic noise of metal clanking guides me over to a small window. I let out a subtle gasp as I realize the cabin is built into the trees. I have the perfect view of the orc, whom I now know as Evrin, as he works on crafting another blade for his bountiful collection.

"A blacksmith," I whisper to myself, sniffling. "Well, Ivy, it's a good thing you know your way around a blade."

I may not be able to take Evrin one-on-one, but at some point, an opportunity to escape will present itself. I will harden my resolve, and by then, I will be ready.

3

EVRIN

I look up towards the swamp canopy; the sun is starting to rise. I've spent the entire night perfecting a new blade for my soon-to-be wife. Last night, when she came running towards me with a blade double her size, it had done naughty things to me. It was clear she has some experience around a sword, but she lacks good form and a well-suited piece of equipment. I plan on rectifying both.

I look down at the carefully crafted dagger in front of me. Halfway through the night, I decided my bride's wedding present needed more decoration. So, I spent hours shaping the metal into a little dragonfly, a creature that reminded me greatly of Ivy. The winged animal represented great change to my people, among many other skills.

I pull away from the dagger to admire my handiwork; the blade is pristine but the ornamentation is leaving much to be desired. Damn, my thick fingers. I grumble to myself. I'm doing a great job of mucking this up.

I sling my hammer against the glowing metal with all my might. Irritation and frustration have eaten away at me all night. I came outside to give both Ivy and myself some reprieve. I needed the distraction. Or else I risked sprinting up to the cabin and rutting my new bride into exhaustion. She's perfect. Too fucking perfect that her mere presence drives me crazy. However, her feelings are not reciprocated. She fears me. Perhaps what's worse is that she just might find me...repulsive. How am I to take an unwilling bride? Will she ever come to love me?

As the thoughts swirl through my mind, the idea of returning her to that squabble is unimaginable. Even if she doesn't forgive me, she deserves a safe home. Something she clearly has yet to experience.

"*I'm not a virgin.*" She'd said those words with such shame, and they perplexed me. Why in the world would I care about such a thing? Then it dawned on me that someone had hurt her. Either her people or the male she laid with, perhaps both. It sent an indescribable fury through me. Even if she doesn't wish to take my hand, I'll never make her return to that place.

I pause my endless hammering and let out a slow breath. I close my eyes and pinch the bridge of my nose, trying to steady my uneasy thoughts. How the fuck am I going to do this? I have to be honest with myself; she may not want to be mine, but will I have the strength to stop myself? Regardless of how I feel about the matter, I'm still trekking her through the dangerous swamps all the way to the Chosen One. I still intend on feeding her the tree's sacred fruit and filling each of her holes until the mating ritual is complete. All while praying that my seed takes root and blesses us with a kit.

"Fuck," I growl. I'm no better than the bastards I took her from. Perhaps I truly am a beast.

I let the few sun rays peering through the mossy branches warm my face. It's time to start our journey. The sooner we leave, the more ground we can cover.

I curse the distance between myself and the Chosen One. We will be forced to camp overnight with so many hidden dangers.

Even if Ivy was an orc, I would still be dangerously protective of her. But the fact she is human only worries me further. Her flesh is round and soft unlike my own, which is thick and hard. A scratch from a thorn is enough to gouge her. The thought of anything harming her makes my blood boil.

I let out a grunt and straighten my spine. She might be the most delectable thing in the swamp, but I am the most dangerous. Anything that attempts to harm my bride will be dealt with swiftly.

I lay down my tools and make my way up the spiral wood staircase I built into the tree. My cabin was never a place of beauty; it was simply a safety precaution so I could rest without the fear of being attacked by one of the swamp's deadly animals. But as I walk the stairs, I feel oddly insecure about my handiwork. When we return to the clan, I will build her the grandest cabin she has ever seen.

My stride falters. The clan.

I've been so caught up in my thoughts of Ivy that it completely escaped me that I would be returning home. My chest suddenly constricts. I'd see my sister and mother again.

All these years, I stopped myself from wondering what the reunion would be like. I thought it was pointless, torturous even. But now, after all these years as an outcast, I've been rewarded with the perfect bride and the ability to return to my people. Not only can I return home, but I can also return proud that I've done my part to sustain another orc generation.

A new fear grips me. My desire for Ivy is driven by selfish motives, yet her approval could reshape the entire destiny of the orcs. Now, more than ever, it is crucial for Ivy to embrace me as her future bridegroom.

I push open the wooden door and step into the small space. Ivy is already awake, sitting in the single chair that occupies the room. She quickly stands, giving me the perfect view of her ample bottom.

She explained to me last night that her current attire wasn't for a wedding, but rather they are her undergarments. I was completely relieved by the confession. But now, as I see her standing in front of me, with all of the curves of her body on display, I can't help but be thankful for my timing.

"*I'd never wear this to my wedding.*" Her words replay in my head, and I silently chuckle. If only she knew.

"Did you get some rest?" I ask, maintaining a safe distance from her. I can't trust myself around her.

"No," she responds honestly, and I can't help the annoyance that piques inside me. I understand why she is restless, but her drowsiness will only be a detriment to herself.

"Listen, I've been thinking," she starts speaking while wringing her hand nervously. "We don't have to do this. You can just let me go. I won't even make you walk me out of the swamps. I can make—"

"Never," I growl, cutting her off. I realize our interactions have been nothing short of aggressive, but that is what happens to an orc who has been an outcast for as long as I have.

"I...I don't understand what you want from me," she cries out exasperatedly.

"Everything." I close the gap between us. "I want you, only *you*, because you were meant to be mine. The gods could send me an entire group of females, and I'd still choose you every time. Your heart, your soul, and your cunt all belong to me. Do you understand?" I bite out, and my declaration sounds more possessive than I intended.

"And did you ever stop and consider what I want?" she shouts. "You orcs might see females as things you can own, but we are so much more than that!"

"Is that why you lived in a rotting house far outside a human village? Tell me, is that how humans truly feel about their women?" I counter. Her disdain for the orcs offends me more than it should. She has every right to hate me, but my actions don't represent my kind.

"I—" She falters. "I would rather go back to that rotting place than be forced to marry a beast."

Her words feel like a slap across the face and her eyes soften as if she just registered the cruelty of her own words. I could explain why I'm a male who's hopeless for his bride. Explain to her why I desperately yearn to see my family and people again. But what good would it do? There is no excuse for my brutish behavior. I simply desire her more than she can possibly imagine. How do I express that I would forsake it all if that meant she could learn to love me? The longing, the possessiveness, the crazed desire. They were all symptoms of something so much bigger than us. I feel it. She is my mate.

My stomach churns. The Chosen One has already blessed our union. All there is left to do is to consummate it. But what if she doesn't feel it? I didn't ask Kal enough questions about his human female, and I greatly regret it. Did she only feel the mating bond after the sacred ritual, or were there signs before that? Fuck, I couldn't let her go even if I tried.

Heavy breathing fills the space between us, and despite my better judgment, I decide to close the gap with a claiming kiss. All these thoughts are fucking with my head, and right now, I just need to feel her touch. Because of our height difference, I lift her up to sit on the edge of the window. I slide my left arm around her waist to make sure she is secure. She lets out a surprised yelp against my lips, and her body goes rigid.

Ivy puts her hands flat against my chest, and I'm

prepared for her to push me away. But instead, she sinks into my embrace. My tusks sink into her round cheeks, feeling at home. The sensation is euphoric.

I pry open her lips with my tongue, and she lets out a moan. My cock, already hard, twitches at the sound. Fuck, her pleasure could sustain me for the rest of my life. My hand finds its way to the back of her head, and my fingers intertwine with her fire-red hair.

With every passing second, I feel her tension slipping away. *Yes, that's it. Accept me. Let me make you feel good,* I silently beg.

I break the connection between our lips and shift my attention to her neck. The desire to mark her with my tusks, claiming her as mine, is overwhelming. Ivy breathes heavily, trying to catch her breath. I lick and lap at the soft part of her neck, deciding that it is the perfect placement to showcase my claim. The sensation of cutting into her fragile skin makes me feel like I can come undone at any moment.

I untangle my right hand from her hair with my left arm still supporting her and begin moving it to the wet spot between her legs. I can smell her arousal, and I want the pain from my tusk to be mingled with her pleasure. Bringing her to a sensation that I know only I can give her.

She shudders under my touch, so meek and giving under my caress. My fingers find the edge of her undergarment, but just as I'm peeling them away, I feel her body go rigid once more.

"No," she breathes.

My exploration of her body, clearly unwelcome, makes me feel sick to my stomach. I immediately back away from her, pulling her out of the window and onto her feet.

Ivy's hand flings to her chest as she struggles to catch her breath. Those sighs and moans are replaced with panic. Something I caused. Fuck.

"Shhh...Ivy, breathe. It's okay." I try to console her without getting too close, as I don't want to frighten her further.

"I-I—" Her anxiety worsens, so in a desperate attempt to ease her pain, I pull her into my embrace.

"Ivy, all you have to do is say no, and I'll never go further. *Never*," I whisper down at her, and her trembling fingers start to wrap around my belt. "I will never hurt you. If you only believe one thing, let it be that."

Her body sinks into mine as her breathing begins to return back to normal.

"Thank you," she whispers, and her soft words make me fucking hate myself. I look up at the ceiling. I'm a pathetic male forever making her feel like this.

"Don't thank me, Ivy," I say, and she pulls back to look up at me. Her brown eyes are so fucking beautiful. "I'm not a good male. I stole you away from your home. I plan on making you travel through the swamp, all with the expectation or hope that you will be mine. All while I declare that your cunt is mine. That I will be the one to fill your womb with my seed," I growl. "But I swear to you...all you have to do is say no, and it is done. Regardless of what words I say or claim, I will not force you. *Ever*. We will walk to the Chosen One, but if you still say no, this will all be over. I'm a selfish male, a brute even. But I'll never force you to accept my touch." I declare the words to her like an oath. I mean every last one of them.

Her lower lip quivers, and a rogue tear slides down her face. I use my thumb to wipe it away, and she nods understandingly. Something has passed between the two of us, and while I'm left with disdain for myself, I hope she feels reassured.

I break our embrace to try and give her some space. "I will make you some leather boots before we leave. They will be ill-fitting, but they will be better than nothing."

"Thank you," she says a little more firmly, and she crosses her arms across her chest.

"We should get going soon; there is a lot of ground to cover before nightfall," I state plainly and leave the room. Every step away from her feels like a stab to the gut. I mull over my promise to her, and I intend to keep it despite knowing that if she rejects me as her mate, it will be a fate worse than death.

4

IVY

We have been walking the entirety of the morning in silence. Evrin isn't a talkative male to begin with, but I know the silence is due to our interaction just before we left.

What had even happened? I should've figured it out by now; I've repeatedly replayed the events in my head. The moment was raw and vulnerable, but perhaps worse, I wanted more. And it terrified me. One moment, I was begging for my freedom, and the next, I wanted to know how Evrin's thick fingers would feel inside of me.

It had all spiraled out of control too quickly. But what happened next surprised me even more. He stopped. No, he comforted me while I panicked, like this little voice in my head could only be sedated by his embrace. And it did.

Ugh. I shake my head to clear my thoughts and continue behind Evrin, trying my best to follow in his giant footsteps. The makeshift boots he made me are too big for my feet, which means stepping in deep mud is a great way to lose them.

Unlike me, Evrin effortlessly treks through the swamp. It makes sense, as he is from this land. But I still can't help but be both envious and annoyed at his grace. I, on the other hand, am extremely clumsy. Normally, I wouldn't classify myself as such, but the mossy, soggy ground is like walking across the ice.

I take a few steps forward, and before I know it, my feet slip from underneath me. I let out a scream, but before I hit the ground, I feel strong hands on my forearms. I look up to find Evrin breathing heavily and staring into my eyes. A moment passes between us, and I swear I can see his eyes flicker to my lips.

I snap out of the haze and find my stability once more. The silence that passes between us has become utterly ridiculous. Evrin has made his intentions known. And I may not have appreciated him stealing me away from my home. However, sad and pathetic it was. I can at least admit to myself that there wasn't much of a house to begin with. He might be dragging me throughout this godforsaken swamp, but at least I know that I won't need a plan to escape. I only need to make it to this Chosen One tree and simply say no. That shouldn't be much of a challenge, should it?

In the meantime, there's no reason we can't at least have a conversation. I know nothing about the male standing in front of me. What are his people like? Why was he living alone? Do all males steal human women?

I decide to break the ice by saying something. "How do you live in such a treacherous place?" I straighten my white undergarments with my hands.

Evrin looks me over to ensure that I am safe enough to continue walking. He turns over my arms to make sure that there are no marks or scratches. I blush under his strict observations. The only thing that is bruised here is my ego.

Once he deems me unharmed he turns to start walking, and at first, I'm afraid he won't respond to my question. Then I realize he is pondering his reply.

"The swamp is both bountiful and unforgiving," he states earnestly. Whatever the fuck that means.

"The human lands don't have anything that will try to kill you?" he asks, and I can see him looking behind his shoulder at me. I smile to myself, knowing that maybe after all this time, he does wanna speak to me.

"Of course there are..." I pause. "Well, I guess the more I think about it, the more I think humans are the most dangerous thing in our land."

"How so?" he asks.

"You are much more at risk from being killed by a human than anything else. In fact, I think it's the other creatures that fear us the most. We tend to have a knack for cruelty."

Evrin slows his stride, falling in place next to me, but only gives a grunt in response to my words. The conversation has turned quite sad quite quickly. Trying to change the subject, I focus on our task at hand.

"Oh no, no, no! You can't walk next to me!" I start pushing against his back to place him in front of me, but he doesn't budge. The male is like an unmovable boulder. Evrin gives me a look of hurt and confusion.

"I can't walk in this mud unless you take steps first. I'm gonna get stuck," I giggle and point down at my little feet. They are not even a quarter of his. Evrin looks down to where I am pointing, and I can see his sudden realization grow across his face in the form of a smile. I can't help but stare at the beautiful expression.

"I can always carry you—"

"Absolutely not!" I cut him off, scolding him. "I will be walking alone, thank you."

Evrin's smile grows wider, but he doesn't protest. Instead, he moves in front of me.

"We will reach more solid ground not very far from her," he yells behind his shoulder.

"Evrin, this is the swamp. I highly doubt that there is such a thing as solid ground."

He bellows in laughter, and the sound startles me. It's unexpectedly captivating. It's almost like the sound fills my core. His laugh is contagious, and I can't help but join in. Suddenly, I feel a tingling sensation between my legs.

Evrin stops abruptly, and his body goes taut as he takes in a deep whiff.

"What is it?" I whisper, fearing danger lurks nearby.

He clears his throat, but he doesn't look back at me for some reason.

"It's nothing," he states firmly and continues on.

Okay, that was odd. We were just having a nice moment before it suddenly became tense. Maybe it's just an orc thing. Yeah, I'm definitely going to use that as an excuse.

"So..." I try to break the silence again, "how come you live alone?"

Evrin grunts and I fear that this topic might not have been the best to address.

"I'm an outcast," he states plainly.

"A what?" I now have even more questions.

"An orc outcast. Don't worry; it's not because of anything that I did." Okay, good, because I was, in fact, worried for a second. "All male orcs are outcasts when they come of age," he continues explaining.

"Wait...all?" I can't believe what I am hearing.

"Yes. All. I've been living out here for years."

Evrin has been giving me grief about my people not appreciating me, but this is so much worse.

"I don't understand. Why?" I extend my hand and grab hold of one of the leather belts, securing his swords on his back, using it to steady myself as we continue to walk. I feel Evrin's muscles tense for a moment before they relax again.

"If you just let me carry—" he starts, but I cut him off.

"Absolutely not! Keep walking."

"You frustrating female," he grumbles.

"Yeah, yeah." I dismiss his comment. "So why do the orcs outcast all the males?"

"Not all the males," he corrects me. "Just the unmarried ones."

He looks over his shoulder and down at me, and I give him a look to continue explaining.

Evrin lets out a sigh. "The orc population is failing. We don't know what causes it. However, over the generations, only male orcs have been born. As you can imagine, this means there are significantly fewer females." He takes a large step over a murky puddle, forcing me to let go of his strap. I feel exposed without his presence. But he quickly turns around and extends his large hand to help me.

But just before I take it, a winged creature lands on the surface of the water, and it is one of the most beautiful things I've ever seen.

"A dragonfly!" I squeal.

I look up at Evrin and find him not staring at the creature but instead staring at me. His lips are upturned, and I feel like I could get lost in his amber eyes.

The winged insect flies off from his brief moment of reprieve to explore the world it calls home.

"I've only ever read about them," I mutter in awe. I stare off into the distance until the creature completely disappears from sight.

"They are beautiful, no?"

"So beautiful," I whisper.

"It may be surprising, but that creature is one of those powerful in the swamp," Evrin explains.

"It is?" I stare at him, perplexed, forgetting that his hand is still stretched out, waiting. I quickly grab onto him and leap over the puddle as he offers an explanation.

"Oh, yes. You see, dragonflies are predators with very few things that eat them. They get to experience the swamp and its beauty without fear. Above all else, they are free. Their wings take them to wherever their hearts desire."

"That must be nice." I ponder his words.

"It is. My people believe they are symbols of good fortune and luck."

"And do you?" I ask, elbowing him. I never took him as somebody who is superstitious. The male I see in front of me is deadly serious.

"I saw one just before I found you. That was the most fortunate moment of my life."

The breath is knocked from my chest at his words. It almost feels like someone is sitting on top of me. Evrin continues walking like his declaration didn't just pierce me to my core.

By the time I regain my senses, I have added a little vigor to my step in order to catch up.

"So before...you were explaining that there are way more male orcs than female orcs." I try to bring the conversation back on topic.

"You ask a lot of questions," Evrin grumbles, and I can't help but smile. I know he is secretly enjoying himself.

"Yes," he continues explaining. "All the males that aren't chosen by orc females by the time we've come of age are sent to live in the swamp as outcasts. We can't return home until we have a bride."

The realization hits me like a ton of bricks. That's why he's so adamant about bringing me to this sacred tree and marrying me. He isn't in love with me; he wants me so he can return home. It feels like my heart is constricting. I know it shouldn't upset me. I've told myself repeatedly since being taken that I wanted to escape. But for a split second, I thought that maybe, just maybe, Evrin truly wanted me for me. That there wasn't an ulterior motive behind his actions.

"Oh," I respond and fall silent. When will I be enough?

I feel my nose begin to tingle, and the urge to cry is overwhelming.

I'm so foolish. I didn't want this. So why does it upset me? Maybe it's because I'm sick of being used by the males of this world. But then I remember why I am being punished by the gods. My father's death on my hands. As a result, I'll never be seen as something worth loving; instead, I'll always be a male's opportunity to get what they want. My mind spirals into endless anxiety, and I don't realize that Evrin has stopped walking, causing me to run into his chest.

When did he turn around?

He grabs me by my shoulders to study me and looks at me deeply in the eyes. "What's wrong?"

"W-what? Nothing," I falter. His question takes me by surprise.

"I can practically hear the gears in your mind turning. Tell me," he presses.

I clamp my mouth shut. I don't like being told what to do, but most of all, I fear that the tears will start streaming down my face.

"Stubborn female," Evrin chuckles under his breath, and I can feel my lip quiver.

He moves his hands from my shoulder and cups my face. I hate how the sensation makes me feel.

"After the ceremony. We will go back to the cabin. I'll build a new hut for us, of course. This one will be much bigger."

Wait, back to the cabin? His words shock me. Wouldn't he want to return to his people?

But as Evrin looks at me, there is a silent understanding. He can sense my anxiety without needing an explanation.

"But don't you have a family?" I cast my eyes downwards.

"I do," he confesses. "I have a mother and a sister. My father died when I was young from sickness."

My stomach drops, and I shake my head, not understanding. "Why would you possibly come back out here?

You'll miss your family. Fuck, you've already been out here long enough."

"I do miss my family...terribly. But unlike before, I'll be able to visit."

"But, but... don't you want to go home?" I can't quite understand his reasoning. He's been an outcast for years. Forced to live all alone. And while the male in front of me is completely capable, I can't imagine how lonely that must have been. He has a family. He has a home. Two things I desperately yearn for. No wonder he stole me away and dragged me into this swamp. I realize that I, too, would do that and much worse if the opportunity presented itself.

Evrin lets out a sigh and leans down to place his forehead on mine. "Ivy, don't you understand? You are my home."

Those words break something in me. A rogue tear trickles down my face. I can feel his hot breath against my lips, and I'm desperate for his touch.

A sudden realization washes over me: Perhaps this wasn't some kind of punishment from the gods. Maybe, just maybe, this was the opportunity I have wanted all my life.

I brush my lips across Evrin's tusks and bring my hand to his, enveloping it. He pulls away from my face and lets our intertwined hands fall to our side. Evrin studies the gesture, like holding hands is unfamiliar to him. Yet he says nothing. Perhaps fearing the moment will end.

I smile, now realizing it is my turn to initiate our hike. Evrin is right; the sooner we get to the Chosen One, the better. Just at the thought, my core tightens in anticipation.

"Tell me more about your family," I prompt as we continue on our journey.

5

EVRIN

"Let me get this straight, metal doesn't occur naturally in the swamp. And since the orcs in the mountains refused to trade with you, you had to enter human territory?" Ivy repeats my explanation just to make sure that she understands. My lips turn upwards. Humans sure like to talk a lot. It's not that I'm complaining; I could listen to her voice for the rest of my life.

My mind quickly turns to a dark place. *"That is if she wants to mate with you."* My heart aches at the thought. No, there's no time for that. All that matters now is setting up camp for the night.

"Yes. You got it," I respond as I scope out an area that will do well enough for the evening.

"I didn't even know there were orcs in the mountains. To be fair, I've never even seen the mountainscape."

"You've never seen the mountains?" I ask, perplexed.

"Nope." She shakes her head. "I've heard about the mountain range from travelers passing by my village, but the northlands are volatile and inhospitable. My people are worried about the swamps."

"Ah yes, you never know what could happen. A big green orc could come and steal you out of your home," I tease, and she slaps me on my arm. Her nose scrunches up, and I have an overwhelming desire to kiss it. But I keep my hands and lips to myself.

"I guess it isn't all that surprising. The mountains are only accessible through the swamps up north."

"So the mountains don't border human lands..." she ponders out loud.

"Exactly. At least the mountain that is occupied by the Zalk."

"The Zalk?"

"An orc clan that lives up the mountains. They are... different from us."

"How so?" She looks up at me with her big brown eyes, and I never want her to stop asking me these questions. Her curiosity is endless. Earlier she asked every possible question about my family. My sister Celia and her mate Olgk. My mother, Jali. It's been so long since I've seen them. Until talking to Ivy about them, I hadn't realized how much I truly missed them. By the gods, they will love her. The last time I heard any news from the village, my sister had three kits, all presumably males.

I shake my head, trying to clear my thoughts away from all the precious moments I've missed. Ivy thinks our people's traditions are cruel, and they wouldn't disagree. Being an outcast isn't about being kind; it's about survival, something we've tried to explain to the Zalk many times.

"Well, for starters, they aren't green."

"Not green? How is that possible?" Ivy is so enthralled in her quest for knowledge that she's just been following me around in circles while I prep our camp for the evening.

"Not green," I chuckle. "They are white. All those years living on the mountain, they've adapted to blend in with the surroundings. I suppose it is the same explanation for why we are green."

"Fascinating," she whispers. "Is that all?"

"No..." I press my lips together hard enough that my tusks protrude into my cheeks. I don't wish to speak ill about our brethren. But over the years, they've become fanatics.

"They don't agree with sending males away from their clan."

"Well, I guess that's understandable. It is fairly...harsh." I notice that she chooses her words carefully. I already know how she feels about my clan's practice, but I appreciate her attempt to hold back in case it upsets me.

"It's not exactly that. You see, they only had an issue with our practice when a male from my clan, Kal, mated and married a human female."

"There are other human females?" She grabs my arm and squeezes tightly.

"Yes, well, just the one. She gave birth to twin girls recently. It's brought a lot of needed hope back to my people," I explain, but she doesn't let go of her tight grip on my arm.

Ah, she is most interested in Kal's mate, Riva. I don't know much about her, other than he caught her in one of his animal traps.

"He stole her too?" She raises an eyebrow.

"We orcs are not very subtle when we want something?" I wince.

"That's the understatement of the century." Ivy rolls her eyes but lets me out of her super grasp.

"Okay, so they don't like interbreeding, got it." She wrings her hands nervously.

"The Zalks are the only ones who feel this way, though. My people love and accept Riva just like they will accept you." My reassurance seems to ease some of her tension.

"Why have we stopped?" She finally realizes we have been looping around in circles in the same open patch of moss.

"It took you long enough," I mutter. "I need to get a hammock set up and a fire going before nightfall and the temperature drops."

"So this is where we are sleeping?" She looks around with uncertainty. I like this about as much as she does, but we have little choice in the matter.

"Hey, look at me." My voice grabs her attention and he stops surveying our surroundings to look up at me. "I'll make sure you are safe. Don't worry. Nothing will get to you."

Ivy lets out a breath of relief. That solidifies it. I need this hammock strung up immediately so I can wrap her in my arms.

"Do you need help with anything?" she asks.

My female is too stubborn for me to say no, that much I know. She wants to feel useful, so let her be useful.

"We need to make a fire. I have some dry felt in my rucksack, but we need peat. There is some over—"

"I know what peat is," Ivy cuts me off and saunters over to the area I was pointing at. She moseys around, trying her best to pretend like she knows what she's doing. I can't help but chuckle as she bends down and starts scooping up mud.

"What's so funny over there?" She scorns me.

"Nothing, nothing. It's just that mud doesn't burn very well."

"I know that. I was just...." She flails for an excuse. "Feeling it. It feels nice."

"Does it?"

"Mhm," she states stubbornly and rubs the mud between her fingers.

I shake my head and can't help the smile that grows across my face. I'm the luckiest male alive. I focus on hanging the hammock between two trees while Ivy pretends like she likes playing in the mud.

"Ah—ha! I found it!" Ivy declares proudly, but as I turn around, I see something truly horrific.

"Ivy, get away from the water!" I scream, but it's too late.

"What?" She stands there, too innocent for her own good as an alligator creeps up the bend.

Ivy screams as the monster lashes out to grab her leg. Luckily, it misses, but she is caught off balance. She is falling backwards and into the—*no*.

Before I can register everything that is happening, I've drawn my sword from my back, and I'm sprinting towards the beast. I hear a splash as Ivy makes contact with the water, and I lunge forward with pure fury. I must protect my mate.

My blade pierces the alligator's top jaw, and with all my might, I drive my sword all the way through the creature's head.

"Ivy!" I scream, leaving the dead beast nailed to the swamp floor. It doesn't matter. There could be more. They could have already gotten her. Fuck, where is she?

She resurfaces, coughing, and I sprint into the bog, disregarding my own safety. We are sitting ducks waiting to be a different creature's next meal. There are more than just alligators in these waters.

"Evrin!" Ivy screams my name like a prayer, and I can feel my heart shattering into a million pieces. I finally reach her, and she grabs onto me with desperation.

"I've got you. I've got you," I repeat the words over and over again for her sake and mine. I drag both of our now soaking bodies out of the water far enough on the land that nothing can sneak up on us.

Ivy continues to cough, desperate to get air back into her lungs.

"Are you okay?" I turn her over, examining every inch of her body.

"I'm sorry, I'm sorry," she repeatedly apologizes.

"Ivy, you have nothing to be sorry for. I failed you. Fuck...I should've never asked you to get that peat," I reprimand myself. I'm disgusted. How could I be so foolish?

"B-but I did find it, didn't I?" Her taunt takes me by surprise. She almost got eaten by an alligator, and she is making jokes?

I let out a chuckle in disbelief. "You infuriating female," I growl, and she gives me a wide grin. I can't help but kiss her. A moment of desperation and fear now quickly turns into passion. She doesn't hesitate to reciprocate. Her mouth is soft and welcoming. She teases my tongue with her own, almost like she is inviting me in. I let out another growl, but this time, it's a lot more threatening. Ivy doesn't know what she is starting. I can't trust myself around her. I'm afraid we are going to begin something that I *demand* we finish.

I let my mind wander back to a few moments ago, the alligator lunging forward and Ivy falling into the water. Those awful memories allow me to gain the strength to pull away from her embrace. But as I pull away, she lets out a little whimper. By the gods, give me the fucking strength to make it through the night.

"You will freeze if I don't set up a fire."

"It's not even that cold," she bemoans.

"That's because the sun hasn't completely set."

I rise to my feet and collect the peat that Ivy dropped before she was attacked. My eyes don't leave her sight as she sits in her soaking white gown. Shame washes over me. She deserves better. A mate that wouldn't drag her through this fucking swamp.

I carry the peat over and set it in a small pile next to her. Her teeth chatter loudly, and I'm frantic to start the fire.

"Hand me the felt out of my rucksack."

"P-please," she chatters.

"What?" I ask, confused. I look over to her, and despite her wet state, she is giving me a crooked smile. She is teasing me once more.

"You didn't say please." She tightens her arms around herself, "Hand me the felt out of my rucksack, *please*," she emphasizes the last word.

Some tension releases in my shoulders at her joking.

"Ah, yes. Can you hand me the felt out of my rucksack, *please*?" I ask.

"Of course I can," she says with a smile.

I can't help the laugh that escapes past my tusks. Ivy similarly wears a smile on her face. Things just feel so easy between us. I'm desperate to make this feeling last forever.

"I apologize for my lack of manners. It's been a while

since I've had a conversation with well...anyone," I try to convey some kind of explanation. As much as I adore Ivy, conversations don't come easily to me. Maybe it's an orc thing.

Ivy rummages through the bag as she responds, "If it makes you feel better, the most company I have had the past four years was with my uncle. And well...you've met him."

My heart sinks at her confession and anger laces my veins. I was never a very social orc, but it's clear Ivy is most definitely a social human.

I make a mental note to seek out Kal on her behalf. That is *if* she decides to take me as her bridegroom. His human mate might make an excellent companion for Ivy.

"What are these?" Ivy asks as she pulls out a napkin of swamp berries. "Sweet berries!" she squeals.

"Is that what humans call them? We call them swamp berries," I chuckle.

"Well...that's what I call them. I don't think many humans even know they exist. They are too close to the swamp," she muses. "I make the best ointment with these!" she declares proudly.

"Ointment?" I ask surprised, "you don't...eat them?"

"Sometimes." She giggles, "but I used them mostly for my uncle's hangovers. Turns out these"—she studies the round blue fruit—"are pretty good at numbing pain."

I try my best to ignore the comment about her worthless uncle, "Really? Orcs just use it to make sweet treats. Not to gloat, but I make the best pies."

"Do you?" She is clearly surprised. "I did not peg you as a baker."

"And why not?" I feign offense.

"I'm just picturing you, a big hulking orc, using your hands for something so delicate," she giggles.

"What can I say? These fingers are very talented." I wiggle them in front of her.

"I bet they are." Ivy's tone drops an octave as she bites her lip. I suddenly get a whiff of her arousal, and my cock immediately hardens. I'm close to letting out a groan when I take in her current state once more. Water droplets drip to the ground, and goosebumps cover her body.

"Fucking her would be the best way to warm her up," something in my brain whispers to me. But I shake away the thought. Not until she accepts me. And while she is clearly turned on, that doesn't mean she wants to take it any further.

As if she read my mind, Ivy clears her throat and refocuses her attention to finding the felt. But instead she pulls out another napkin-wrapped item.

"What's this?" Ivy muses as she begins unwrapping. *Fuck*. The dagger I made her. That was supposed to be a surprise after we were mated.

"Nothing—" I try to reach over, but she had already revealed it. I close my eyes and take a deep breath to calm my nerves.

"By the gods, it's beautiful!" She stares at the wedding gift in awe. "Did you make this?"

"Yes," I whisper. Her appreciation of my craftsmanship softens something in me, "It was supposed to be a surprise."

"For what?"

"For our wedding," I state plainly. "It's for you."

Her eyes widen in shock as she looks between the dagger and me. Silence threatens to strangle me.

"I don't understand," she finally responds.

"I made it last night. When you drew that sword on me in the cabin, I noticed it was too heavy for you. I wanted you to have something that fit your size and would enhance your skill set."

"The dragonfly..." she croaks, and I fear I've upset her.

"It doesn't just represent good luck but also strength and freedom. I know we don't know each other well, but they remind me of you."

Tears suddenly start flooding her eyes, fuck. That's

it, I fucked up. She hates it. I want to reach out to her as a gentle sob escapes her lips, but I fear I've done enough damage. I look down at the mossy ground in shame but suddenly feel an arm wrap around my shoulders.

It takes me a few moments to realize Ivy is embracing me, but I finally wrap her in my arms to console her.

"Thank you," she sobs into my neck. Clearly, something more is happening, but I don't press her. I just hold her as she cries.

"Of course, my love," I whisper into her ear.

"S-sorry." She lets out a pitiful laugh as she tries to control her tears.

"Never apologize for your feelings, Ivy. Tell me, what upsets you?"

"It's foolish," she tries to dismiss her feelings.

"Your feelings are anything but foolish," I state firmly. She searches my eyes, and I hope that she can tell that I am earnest.

"My father was the one who taught me how to handle a sword," she shares and looks down at her fingers. My confident, carefree human suddenly feels very nervous about sharing this part of her story. I tighten my grip around her waist and listen carefully to her words.

"He died when I was young. He was killed on a

mercenary trip that he took with my uncle. We were desperate for money, and my dad was determined to take care of me. So, despite my uncle's protests, they took a dangerous job," she continues. "My uncle and my father were the best of friends. They were inseparable." She lets out a painful laugh, and I fear the tears are about to return. "He took it the hardest when my dad was killed. Turned to the bottle. In a way, it's like he is dead, too. Simply a shell of his former self."

My heart hurts for her. To lose a parent at such a young age is heartbreaking, I would know. I, too, lost my father.

"And your mother?" I ask hesitantly.

"She died in childbirth with me." She swallows. "So you see, I've killed everyone I've ever cared about." I feel her break in my arms, and her pain makes me sick to my stomach.

I pull her away from my shoulder and cup her face. "Ivy, listen to me; you did not kill your family!" I state firmly. The mere idea that she even believes that destroys me. I think back to our first meeting, and her words replay in my head.

"I've killed enough people in my family."

I curse under my breath. I didn't understand what she meant then. That's why she came to me so willingly.

"Ivy, look at me." She does her best to avoid eye

contact, but my hands keep her firmly in place. "You did not kill anyone in your family. Do you understand?"

"But—" she tries to deny it, but I am quick to cut her off.

"There are no buts. Your mother's death, while tragic, was a cruel accident. Your father knew the risks. While he may have been trying to provide for you, that in no way makes you responsible. And your uncle, well, I don't have many nice words for that male," I growl. "While I can sympathize for the loss of his brother, to blame a child is utterly unacceptable."

Her lip quivers, and she lets out more uncontrollable sobs. Like she had been waiting for someone her whole life to tell her that she wasn't the one responsible. Fuck, it makes me murderous. If we didn't have to make it to the Chosen One, I would trek through this swamp and make that pathetic male who calls himself her uncle pay.

"Is that why he had you living outside of town? As some kind of punishment for your father's death?" I ask, horrified that he would punish her in that way.

Ivy shakes her head, no, and I'm left perplexed.

"But why would—"

"That's also because of me," she whispers, ashamed. A few moments of silence pass until she gathers her strength. "I told you before that I am not a virgin."

My heart sinks to my stomach. Surely, her kind wouldn't punish her for this simple fact. But I was wrong.

"His name was Sorin. Turns out he was a scam artist. He travels to towns, making young, foolish women fall in love with him, and convinces them to run away, all in a ploy for them to bring him money."

I can't fathom what I am hearing, so I stay silent as my blood begins to boil.

"I just so happened to be one of these foolish women. I was desperate for someone to love me. I was the perfect target. I gave him my virginity willingly, thinking that as soon as we ran away, we would be married. I was so unbelievably wrong." She laughs humorlessly to herself. "Long story short, he convinced me to steal my uncle's savings and then promised to meet me at the swamp's edge. Needless to say, he never showed up."

I grind my teeth together, and I feel my tusks dig into my cheeks. I will find this male and dismember him.

"Humans only value females by their purity. So, when I lost my virginity out of wedlock, my uncle and I were shunned by our community. That's why we lived so far from the town." Her voice is barely above a whisper as she focuses on the ground.

"Ivy..." I growl.

"Are you mad at me?" she breathes, and I see tears falling to the mossy floor.

"Fuck no." I put my finger under her chin to lift her face to mine. "I'm mad, no, I'm fucking furious, but not at you. At that worthless male who took advantage of you. At the humans that outcasted you for simply seeking pleasure, and at your worthless uncle who should've honored his brother's death by protecting you," I grind out my words, trying my best not to let my anger get the best of me.

"Thank you," she murmurs, and her nose wriggles with a little sniffle.

I sigh. "You don't need to keep thanking me for the bare minimum. You don't have to ever thank me for anything—" Ivy cuts off my sentence with a kiss.

One moment, I'm fueled with rage, but now I'm fueled by something much more sinister. I can't stop the groan that escapes my chest as she takes her time exploring my mouth with her soft mouth. After a few moments of panting and moaning, she finally feels satisfied to pull away. Already, I miss her lips, but I am pleased at the sight of their puffiness.

She shifts from my embrace and places her small hand in mine. "The felt." She hands over the fire starter and giggles. How long has she been holding on to that? I cast the question away and refocus on tending to my mate.

With the felt finally on top of the pile of peat, I strike a few rocks together to start a spark. Before I know it, the flame illuminates Ivy's beautiful round cheeks. She blushes under my gaze, which makes my cock twitch. She focuses on the flame, sticking out her hands in order to warm herself.

"You know, it's funny," she prompts.

"What is?" I ask.

"This place is meant to be a death sentence for humans, and yet I feel so free."

My smile crooks upwards; perhaps there is hope that she will mate with me. But instead of pushing her any further, I simply say, "Warm-up, my little dragonfly."

...

"I D-DON'T KNOW how I feel about this." With her teeth still chattering, Ivy takes another bite into the dried piece of meat I handed to her for dinner. Despite sitting next to the fire, her clothes are taking an awfully like time to dry. I curse the swamp's humidity. Even at night getting things to dry is terribly difficult.

"I know, little dragonfly, but it's all the food I have at the moment. You need to eat in order to be strong," I coax her into taking another bite. Forget being strong. I want to scoop her up, strip her naked, and warm her up.

"Do you have any more of the sweet berries?" She gives me her best fake smile. Doesn't she know by now that those big brown eyes will get her anything she wants so long as nature permits it? Unfortunately for her, right now, nature is a bitch.

"Those were the first things we ate," I tease her.

"Ug, I know, but they are so good!" she whines, and I can't help but laugh. She insisted that I eat the berries as well so she didn't feel guilty hogging all of the "good" food.

Ivy scoots forward to get herself closer to the fire.

"Ow!" she screeches and jumps back.

"What? What is it?!" I ask, alarmed.

"Nothing, nothing." She waves me off. "I just hit a hot coal." She grabs her foot and studies her big toe. Still shivering, she attends to the burn without complaining. That's it, I can't take it anymore. She needs to warm up.

"This is ridiculous," I growl.

"W-what is?" she asks, confused.

"You're freezing with your wet clothes still on. They are most likely going to take all night to dry," I state plainly.

"I'm o-okay. I promise." She tries to brush off her discomfort but I've witnessed first hand just how uncomfortable she is.

"No, you're not, Ivy. You just stuck your foot in the fire to get some warmth. I've watched you shivering all evening," I scold her for being dishonest. There is no reason to suffer, except I know why she is hesitant to complain. She doesn't want to get naked. And while I would respect her wishes, letting her die of hypothermia or getting sick is not an option. I have no other choice but to be the bad orc she has always thought me to be.

"Take off your clothes." I stand.

"W-what?" she gasps.

"Ivy." I brush a hand over my face. "You can't stay in those wet clothes. You are going to get sick. I promised not to let anything bad happen to you, and believe it or not, the best way to keep that promise is if you take off your clothes."

"How convenient for you," she grumbles.

"I'll turn away, and you can climb into the hammock."

Ivy looks at me and then to the hammock. "But there is only *one* hammock..."

"I'll stay awake and tend to the fire. Don't worry." I

had hoped we would cuddle, but that was before she fell into the water.

"But it's *your* hammock. You should sleep in it. I can stay by the fire." She tries to compromise, but I'm not having it.

"That's out of the question. It's not safe to sleep on the swamp floor. There are too many dangers, and it's too damp. I don't think you understand me; you are going to undress, and you are going to sleep in that hammock. That's final," I growl.

It's Ivy's turn to stand; she puts her hands on her hips and squares up to me. Stubborn female. She is maybe half my size but doesn't shrink under my presence. Fuck, her defiance is making me so hard.

"You are not the boss of me." And before I can respond, she is stripping off her clothes. First, her white frilly shorts and then her white billowy top. Ivy's creamy skin is exposed, so suddenly, I don't know where to look. Her pink nipples pucker as they make contact with the air. I can't stop my eyes from wandering further down until they reach her ginger sex. A groan escapes me, and that seems to please her. Ivy has won this little victory, and she knows it.

I try my best to compose myself by looking up to the sky and praying to the gods for strength. But as I hear Ivy begin to walk away, I take a glimpse at her generously large backside. She is shaped like the pears that grow in my clan's village. So round and juicy. My mouth begins to water at the sight.

Ivy saunters slowly to the hammock, but it's too far away from the fire to see anything too explicit. I curse under my breath and cup my dick. I need relief, and I need it quickly. It's decided once she has fallen asleep, I'll be able to diligently tend to my aching cock.

I pick up her wet clothes from the ground and start setting up some rope to hang over the fire.

"What are you doing?" I hear Ivy's voice call out from the hammock.

"Hanging up your wet clothes," I respond. And thinking about your ample breasts. But I decide to keep that last part to myself. "What are you doing?" I ask.

"Thinking..." she muses.

Okay, now I'm intrigued.

"Thinking about what?"

"Thinking about how I'm still cold," she whines. "Maybe you could help warm me up?"

I stand there in stunned silence. This is bad. No, this is amazing. But also *very* bad. I have no self-control around this human. I finish hanging her flimsy clothes on the rope and think of a response.

"And how would I do that?" I ask carefully.

"You were so warm when you were holding me

earlier. And you don't have a place to sleep—" Before she can finish her sentence, I've shed both my swords and clothes and started climbing into the hammock. Like I said, no self-control.

Ivy lets out a squeal. "Are you naked?!"

"I thought it was only fair," I tease her as I scoop her up so I can find a good spot in the hammock.

"Gods, you're so warm," she moans, and I know she is being sincere. She is colder than I thought. Her skin is fucking frigid.

"Ivy, you should have told me if you were this cold," I scold her, pulling her back to lay on top of me. I move over my bulging hard-on to make room for her body.

"Don't be mad at me. You get to warm me up now." She pokes my chest. If she feels my cock, she hasn't said anything.

"Well, if I knew that this was an option, I would have demanded you get naked much sooner," I flirt, and she slaps me.

"You are so bad!" she giggles, and that sound is the most perfect noise I've ever heard. I never want this moment to end. Her in my arms, us laughing—it just feels so perfect.

"So...if you return to your clan, would you still be a blacksmith?" Ivy asks. My mind ruminates on the words "*if*" and "*your*." There are still doubts about a potential life together. I do my best to stop it from ruining this moment. For if she only wants me to hold her for this one night, I'll be the luckiest orc who has ever lived.

"Yes. The clan still needs weapons. They are broken quite frequently—ahhhhh." My words are replaced with a groan as Ivy wraps her small hands around my throbbing member.

"Fuck," I grind out, and she slides her hand up my shaft ever so slightly. "Ivy," I whisper almost as a warning.

"Does that feel good?" she asks, and her voice is so soft I can't barely hear it.

"So fucking good," I moan.

"You are so big," she sighs.

"Mhm, do you like the size of my orc cock?"

"*Yes*," she says breathlessly.

"Fuck it. Come here," I growl and pull her on top of me. "Sit on my face. I've smelled your arousal for long enough. I need to know what you taste like."

Ivy remains quiet, but shimmies her way up my body until her pretty pussy dangles over me.

"Hang on, my little dragonfly," I warn, and as soon as I know she holds on to a tree branch, I bury my face into the most delectable meal of my life.

"Fuck!" Ivy screams as I lap at the little bud at the top of her sex. It seems to be extremely sensitive, so I take my time to coax a response from her. Our moans mingle, and I can feel my cock leaking pre-cum.

Ivy grinds her cunt against my left tusk, and by the sound and rhythm of her screams, I know she is getting close.

She leans back, reaching for my cock, but I stop her.

"What's wrong?" she asks, gasping for air.

"Absolutely"—I give her another lick—"nothing." But I can hear the apprehension in the silence so I offer a better explanation. "I don't want to come just yet."

"Why?!" she whines.

"Because when I come, it's going to be deep in your womb," I growl and return to eating her soaking wet pussy.

"Fuuuckkkkk, Evrinnn," Ivy lets out a growl of her own. It would seem like my words only heightened her pleasure. Does my little human want me to breed all three of her pretty holes?

Ivy slumps over to catch her breath. Finally, the events of the past few days have caught up with her. She is exhausted. I wrap my arm around her waist and pull her back down to lie across my chest. I can feel her heart beating rapidly and her chest rising and falling. Still, she remains silent, and that fucking terrifies me.

"You are sweeter than swamp berries, little dragonfly." That earns me a giggle, and relief washes over me.

"Let me make you feel good," Ivy grumbles sheepishly.

"You already have." I lean down and place a kiss on the top of her head. "Tonight is about you."

She doesn't respond. I wait a few more minutes until I feel her breathing rhythmically deepen. She is asleep.

I pull her into my body ever so slightly out of a protective instinct. I won't get a wink of sleep tonight. I want to cherish every second of this. Because tomorrow we will arrive at the Chosen One. Tomorrow, she could very well reject me as her mate. Tomorrow, my world could come crumbling down.

6

IVY

The night came and went. Before I knew it, we were already traveling through the thick swamp bush. I awoke this morning with a new lease on life. Our journey to the Chosen One wasn't merely a task that I was being forced to complete before returning home. Now, it's so much more. It is my destiny, my freedom, and most importantly...my future.

I look down at my dragonfly dagger and instinctively smile. It is the most thoughtful gift I've ever received. "*My little dragonfly,*" Evrins's new endearment for me. I absolutely love it. And now that I know what this little insect represents, it has quickly become my favorite creature within the swamp—perhaps second favorite creature after the orcs.

I look up to face Evrin's strapping back. I still follow behind to retrace his footsteps to avoid getting stuck in mud. After yesterday's events, he is extra cautious. One might describe him as overly protective. Not that I can blame him. The idea of him being harmed by anything makes my stomach churn. I rub my hand over my chest to soothe the aching feeling. It's as if the mere thought of being without him causes my body to react.

So many things have changed between us in such a short amount of time. I once saw him as a beast sent from the gods to punish me. Little did I know that he was there to save me. And maybe, just maybe I've saved a little piece of him too.

We've both been through so much. But with him, I somehow feel stronger. When Evrin told me I wasn't to blame for my circumstances, I actually believed it for the first time in my life.

Now, we travel to our new future—to the Chosen One. There, he is to make me his wife. The thought makes my core tingle, and I can feel my shorts begin to moisten.

Evrin's steps falter briefly before he regains his stride. It is now clear to me that he can smell my arousal. The fact that mortified me at first now interestingly turns me on.

"I thought you said that we would be arriving in the

early afternoon," I shout so he can hear me.

"Yes, but I may have been a little eager for that estimate," Evrin says over his shoulder.

"We've been hiking for ages. I swear we've passed that tree with the funky trunk about three times," I chuckle, but I have no sense of direction. I pause and study the unique vining across the branches. The swamp is so fascinating. Everything feels so alive. It's bountiful in well...everything. It's almost as if it calls to me. I wander off the path slightly and notice the moss has been stomped down. My heart thrums as I place my hand along the vining.

"Ivy," Evrin barks, and it startles me.

"Ow!" I snatch back my hand from the vines and study where my fingernail just carved out a small mark after being spooked.

"Get away from there before you get hurt," he says in a more gentle tone, but I notice how his spine and shoulders are straightened. Oddly, it's almost as if he is...defensive.

"To answer your question, we are walking slower since you won't let me carry you. Come on, you don't want to get lost." Evrin quickly brings the conversation back on topic.

I shake off my nerves. "You carried me this morning!

If I remember correctly, my kisses were slowing us down then, too."

"Yes, well, that's far more enjoyable than this kind of slow walking," Evrin grumbles.

I laugh under my breath. If it was up to him, we would've taken breaks every mealtime so he could, as he likes to say, "feast on my pussy". Funnily enough, it's me who has become the impatient one.

To me, it was more than just being mated to Evrin; I was also excited to belong to a village. It has been so many years since I was last welcomed into mine. Hopefully, what Evrin says is true, and they like me. I'm particularly intrigued to meet Kal's mate. Apparently, she is a human, just like me.

Recounting my story to Evrin made me realize just how lonely I've been all these years, not only for a partner but also for friends and family. But he has those things, and soon, so will I. The thought energizes me and they had a little pep to my step.

"Let's pick up the pace, slowpoke!" I jog past Evrin in my oversized boots.

"Ivy, slow down! Let me walk in front of you," he demands.

"Oh, come on! Quit your worrying. I defeated an alligator yesterday, remember?" I tease.

"No," Evrin growls, "I defeated the alligator while you nearly drowned."

"Semantics," I scoff.

"Infuriating female," Evrin grumbles, and I can't help but giggle. I love teasing him; he is far too easy to rile up. The male doesn't complain about anything except my safety. I'm not proud to say that I enjoy being his weakness far too much. I can only imagine how he will be with our children.

The thought stops me in my tracks, and I instinctively graze my hand across my stomach. I haven't thought of being a mother in a long, long time. It was always too painful. Like a treat being dangled in front of a child who knew they could never have it. But now...it's well within my grasp.

"Ivy?" Evrin gently touches my cheek. "Are you okay?"

When did he catch up to me? I didn't realize I had stopped walking; I was too caught up in thought.

"Yes." I smile. "Just thinking."

"About what?" He shifts nervously on his feet.

"Nothing, just getting hungry." I don't know why I lie; maybe it's because of my nerves. The orcs outcast all these males just so they can breed offspring. They are particularly desperate for females. But...what if I don't give him a daughter? Only sons. Or worse, we can't have children at all.

"I can see worry on your face, little dragonfly." He caresses my cheek. "Tell me."

"Your clan sends you out here so you find someone to reproduce, right? What if it doesn't work?" I ask nonchalantly. I'm not ready to share my insecurities. I know he would simply reassure me, but I don't want to be consoled. I want the truth.

I watch his jaw tick as he chooses his words carefully. "Orc seed is very fertile."

There is suddenly unspoken tension between us, and I don't know why. Perhaps both of us are too stubborn for our own good, but neither one of us will be the first to spill the beans. So instead I opt to redirect our focus by continuing our journey.

I reach my arms up and stand there expectantly. "Well? Are you just going to stand there, or are you going to carry me?"

"Ah, is that what that means?" he chuffs.

"Mhm," I coo, and then I squeal as he scoops me up in his arms. "You said we are going slow because you can't carry me, so I am expecting top speeds from here on out."

"Is that right?" Evrin raises an eyebrow at me.

"Yes, or I'll have to use this." I pull out my wedding

present and point it at him, earning me a booming laugh. The way his ponytail sways as he smiles makes my heart skip a beat. This male is no beast. He is the most magnificent creature I've ever laid eyes on.

"Okay, okay, I promise," he concedes. "Just be careful with that thing."

"Good. I'm glad we are on the same page." I wave my dagger around like a wand. "Now march."

"As you command," he whispers into my ear, and we are off once more.

...

"No way!" I gasp at Evrin's story. "She beat you up? But you are so"—I wave at his massive body—"big."

"Believe it or not, I haven't always been this big. She is my older sister, and at that time, she was bigger than me—and stronger, too." He shakes his head, like he is reliving the memory.

"Well, serves you right. You let a pig loose in her bedroom," I say exasperatedly. "Where did you even find a pig? Do they live in the swamp?"

"We have wild hogs. Orcs domesticated them a while ago. Our farmers usually tend to them, but I was young and got a tad bit carried away," he states plainly

"Wait..." It takes me a few minutes to understand what he was admitting. "You stole the pig?!"

"Oh yeah," Evrin says while laughing, "my sister was

just the first orc to get their hands on me."

I laugh alongside him and snuggle deeper into his arms.

The sun is starting to set. We've been walking—well, Evrin has been walking while he carries me—and talking. I love hearing about his childhood. I even divulged some of my happiest memories with my father.

But as happy as our journey has made me, I'm desperate to reach our destination.

"Evrin..." I bat my eyelashes.

"Don't tell me you have to pee again," Evrin grumbles.

"I'm sorry! I can't help it." I giggle. "I'll be quick, I promise. Besides, I need to stretch my legs."

"If it was up to me, you'd never have to use your legs again."

"Oh, I know, big guy"—I pat his shoulder"—but I quite like using my legs. Thank you very much."

"Very well," he sighs and places me back on my feet.

I use Evrin's arm to stabilize myself and let out a big stretch. My bladder is full, and if I laugh any more, I risk peeing all over him.

"I'll be right over here," I shout as I walk over to a spot that isn't too far away but gives me a little bit of privacy to relieve myself.

"Be quick," Evrin warns; he never likes when I am too far away.

"Always am." I give him a wink and tend to my business.

While relieving myself, I take in my swampy surroundings. The greenery is cast in a golden haze from what I can only presume is the sunset. The dense canopy over the swamplands makes it difficult to see the bright sky, but pockets of sunshine peek through.

Suddenly, something catches my eye. I finish peeing and pull up my shorts to go quietly investigate.

This area looks oddly familiar, again, the wonky tree. I squint my eyes and shake my head. The swamp all looks the same to me. There have been dozens of wonky trees; surely it isn't the same.

But the closer I get, something small begins to appear—the nick I made in the vines earlier when Evrin startled me.

I brush my hand over the gash. No, this can't be. We must be lost or some other explanation. No way could Evrin know we have been walking around in circles. We are making our way to the Chosen One. I feel my stomach hollow out as something in me prompts me to push away the vines and reveal a pathway illuminated by an unfamiliar luminescent glow. I know right then and there what it leads to without moving any further. This is the Chosen One, and we arrived hours ago.

"Ivy," Evrin whispers my name.

Tears well in my eyes at his betrayal. He doesn't want to marry me. He doesn't want...a rogue sob escapes my lips. Ivy, you fucking fool. Evrin tries to close the gap between us, but I stick out my hand. "Stay away from me."

"Ivy, let me explain," he pleads.

"You lied to me!" I shout. "This whole time, you led me to believe we weren't even close; meanwhile, we've been walking around for hours when it was right here!"

"I shouldn't have—" he starts, but I can't bear to hear his excuse

"You don't want to mate with me?" I say rather pathetically as more tears roll down my face

"It has nothing to do with that!" Evrin growls and once again tries to reach out to me, but I instinctively back away. I am terrified of his touch because I know just how much power it has over me. My panic starts taking over as I have a flashback to that frightful night near the swamp four years ago. It is happening all over again, except this time it's with someone I shared all of my vulnerabilities with. I can't control my breath, can't control my tears...I feel like...I can't breathe.

Evrin bridges the gap between us, and I desperately

claw to get away from him, but his arms hold me in place.

"Stop it!" he growls. "Listen to me, don't you ever fucking think I don't want you. Ever, do you understand me?"

He's confusing me. "Then why?" I cry out. "Why haven't you taken me to the Chosen One?"

"Because I'm scared to lose you!" he shouts, and the sudden silence threatens to consume us. Evrin lets out an exasperated sigh, and his voice sounds almost defeated. "Ivy, you are the best thing that has ever happened to me. I knew from the first moment I held you in my arms that you were my mate. Not just a bride I would take to the Chosen One but my *mate*. I know that doesn't mean much to you, and as a human, I don't even know if you feel the same way. I don't blame you for that; I just..." He leans down and places his forehead on mine. "I can't live without you. But I refuse to be your jailer any longer. You deserve the happy life that you chose. Not because an orc beast stole you away."

"Mate? Like an invisible force that draws you to another? The feeling like someone is sitting on your chest. Desperate to be in their presence and in their company? Evrin, I know exactly what that feels like," I cry out, frustrated. "Why would you ever think I wouldn't choose you?"

"Because this entire time, you've always said things like '*your clan*' and '*if we mated.*' I just..." A rogue tear rolls down his handsome green face. "Just wanted to spend more time with you before you decided to leave."

My heart constricts at his confession, and the more time that passes, the more I realize what he says is true. My feelings have changed over the past few days, but I haven't spoken about them due to my own fears.

I place my hands on his cheeks and pull him in for a demanding kiss. He reciprocates fiercely, and both of us ravage each other's mouths like it will be the last time. Our sadness, confusion, anger all mingle into one as we explore each other's bodies.

"I chose you," I cry out in between kisses. "I love you so fucking much."

"Fuck, my little dragonfly. So do I. I love you the way the sun loves the moon. The way day craves the night. I love you endlessly and desperately, Ivy. I will spend the rest of our days making this up to you. I promise." Evrin picks me up by my ass and carries and pushes me against the wonky tree; his raging boner digs into my belly, and I let out a moan. I need him inside of me desperately.

"Then take me. Make me yours forever," I breathe into his lips and give his tusk a little lick.

"Oh, I fucking plan to," he barks, "but this won't be like last night. This claiming will be much...rougher."

I reach out to find his throbbing cock and give it a tight squeeze.

"Prove it," I challenge.

Evrin lets out the most possessive growl I've heard him make, and before I know it, we are barreling down the path to the Chosen One.

7
IVY

I don't have time to take in my surroundings, nor do I care. All I want right now is to feel Evrin's hands all over my body. To feel his cock stretch me open. I attend diligently to his lips as we kiss like there is no tomorrow. Both of our breaths are heavy, and I have no sense of direction. First, there is darkness, and then there is a faint...glow.

The intensity of the light grows with Evrin's every step. I pull away from him for a slight reprieve and to regard the great tree that lies before us. I don't have to ask; this is the Chosen One.

Its thick roots span across a tiny isle ensconced in velvety grass. Where most of the water in the swamp is murky, the water surrounding the Chosen One is crystal clear. More interesting are the purple luminescent veins throughout the tree trunk. I can feel its presence like it is a living, breathing thing.

Willowy vines with hundreds and thousands of pinkish purple leaves grow from various branches, making them almost look like hair. But that is not all; there is something growing, almost like...fruit?

I squint my eyes to get a better view. Round, luscious purple fruits grow along the slender tendrils. My mouth waters at the sight of them. Their beauty beckons me, and I've never been so compelled to eat something in my entire life.

"I-I can't even describe what I'm seeing right now," I whisper in awe.

"Now you know how I feel every time I look at you." Evrin pushes back a loose strand of hair behind my ear. I turn back and look at him, and a sense of certainty and anticipation consumes me. Nothing has ever felt so right, so why am I nervous? Perhaps because to be loved wholly and truly can only be done if you love yourself. I've spent my entire life thinking I was a scourge. That I was destined to be unhappy. But now? I realize I was just one of many people in the world who were subjected to unfair circumstances. That others taking advantage of you is a reflection of their own self-hatred. Not my own. It only took a hulking orc to make me realize it. I'm done being afraid to love. I'm done making myself smaller in order to be palatable to others. I deserve love, happiness, and a family. Most importantly, I deserve to forgive myself.

"Do you crave it?" Evrin asks.

"What?" I shake my head to clear any final self-doubt.

"The fruit. Do you crave its sweet taste like I crave you?" Evrin mumbles against my neck, using his tongue and tusk to tease my most vulnerable spot.

"Mhm," I moan as he wades us through the clear water to reach the Chosen One's special island.

"I want you so fucking much I can't even think straight," he grumbles and pushes me against the trunk of the tree.

"I can't wait any longer. You once told me that all I have to say is no. That you would back off without any questions asked. Well, I don't want to say no. I want you. I'm saying yes, Evrin," I plead and kiss him frantically. "Take me. Make me yours."

"I will. In due time, my little dragonfly," he promises in a husky voice, "but first we must feast."

He gently lays me down at the base of the tree before he walks over to one of the willowy branches and plucks one of the round fruits.

"Take off your clothes," he mutters as he studies my plump body.

"Maybe I want you to take it off for me," I tease, and my pussy tingles when I see his grip tighten around the fruit.

"Ivy," he growls, "it's either you take your clothes off intact, or I'll rip them to shreds trying to get to your cunt."

Evrin's gentle nature is fraying with every second. I watch his chest rise and fall dramatically as he tries to control his urges.

"Destroy them, I don't give a fuck" I almost say out loud, but I bite my tongue. I'm still in a clear enough consciousness to realize I have no other clothing options. As much as I want to be naked for Evrin, I don't want to be naked for our clan.

Our clan, the word is so simple yet so meaningful. Finally, I will belong. And most importantly, I will be loved.

My big floppy boots and dagger are the easiest things to remove, I throw them off to the side but make sure to take off my clothes with purpose.

"It's only fair if you take off your pants as well," I say, slipping off the strap of my white tank top.

"As you wish, my bride," he responds, unlacing his trousers with his free hand.

I can see the outline of his cock; when he notices me staring, I swear to the gods I can see it twitch.

I lick my lips as my top flutters to the ground. Evrin growls at the sight of my large tits. I cup both of them in my hands, bring one close enough to my mouth, and give it a lick.

"Infuriating, female," Evrin gripes. "Why do you tease me so?"

I giggle, but when he pulls down his brown leather hide covering his growing member, it is my turn to growl.

Last night was the first time I *felt* how big he was, but to *see* it was something else entirely. He is *massive*.

A gasp escapes my lips, both from slight fear and intrigue. How the fuck is that going to fit inside any of my holes? Let alone one.

"Do you like what you see, little dragonfly?" he asks.

"Mhm." I nod and bite my lip.

I push off my shorts, and he gives his shaft a tight squeeze. I am not completely exposed, the only article of clothing which remains are my black stockings. It's like we are playing a dangerous game of cat and mouse. Only it's very clear who is the predator and who is the prey.

"Come here," he commands, and I saunter over. His eyes don't leave my breasts, and he strokes himself a few times. More liquid seeps from his green mushroom-like head than I've ever seen. I can only imagine what it will look like when I bring him to an orgasm. I clench my thighs together at the thought, and Evrin inhales deeply.

"Female, you are driving me insane." He studies my body like a piece of art, and I feel utterly worshiped by his gaze.

He leans down and whispers in my ear. "If I reach down, am I going to find your pussy soaking wet?"

On command, a droplet of my own wetness rolls down my left thigh. Before I have time to react, Evrin bends down and licks it up like he hasn't eaten for days before standing once more.

"I take that as a yes," he says, gently kissing my lips so I can taste myself.

"You are right," I giggle, "I am sweet."

"Yes, you are," he groans. "Now open that pretty little mouth. Let me feed you."

"Only if I can feed you," I demand.

"Fair enough," he says, breaking the fruit in half and handing me a portion. "The fruit is a product of the Chosen One. After we consume its bounty, it will determine if we are suited mates. We will be either ignited with passion or fueled with animosity."

I let out a shaky breath. I didn't fully anticipate the high stakes. I take a moment to regain my strength. I have nothing to worry about. Evrin is my mate, and nothing will ever change that.

I open my mouth and wait for fruit to touch my tongue. But all I feel is Evrin's thick fingers slowly making their way to the back of my throat.

I gag upon reflex, and he sighs, "Fuck, it's so tiny. Your throat is going to feel like heaven on my big orc cock."

"I don't know if I can take it all," I whimper.

"You will. Maybe not today or tomorrow, but we will train all of your tight holes to take all of me."

My pussy is soaking wet at our exchange, and I can see his pre-cum dripping onto the grass. My mind flicks back to the memory of him explaining how fertile orc sperm is. Looking around at the bountiful isle, I can only wonder if it's because of the magic here.

Finally, Evrin's fingers return to my mouth, but this time with the fruit. I let out a long moan as the juices spread across my tongue. It's the most delectable thing I've ever tasted.

I reciprocate the exchange and bring up my half to Evrin's mouth. He takes a deep bite and lets out a moan of his own. It doesn't take long for the tree's effect to take over.

My lust compounds into unquenchable desire. I feel like I've been possessed, and by the look in Evrin's amber eyes, he, too, feels the effects.

"Get on your fucking knees," he growls and I do as he commands.

Without hesitation, I wrap my small hand around his massive cock. He lets out a guttural moan as I lick from the base of his balls all the way to the tip.

My mouth is already full with his pre-cum, and it's utterly delicious. I make sure to swallow it whole and my pussy clenches in anticipation. Soon, I will be filled to the brim with his seed.

"That's it, take my cock in your tiny human mouth." Evrin's aggressive words only excite me more.

First, the tip of his dick slides neatly across my tongue. The ridged underside of the mushroom-shaped head seems to be the most sensitive, so I make sure to tease it slightly.

Evrin is panting not only from pleasure but from forcing himself to hold back. I look up at him with my big brown eyes as he studies my cock-stuffed mouth. I've only taken half of him, and up to this point, we have gone slow.

I can see his tusks dig into his cheeks. Something that only happens when his jaw is clenched tightly. With his swords strapped to his back, he looks so unbelievably sexy and utterly dangerous. Gone is the doting, gentle male; all that is left is pure beast. But instead of fearing him, I want this creature to plow me until I can't walk straight.

Perhaps it is the fruit or maybe the spur of the moment, but a new sensation grips my body. Pain does not exist here, only pleasure.

I relax my jaw and open my mouth even further to let him sink down my throat even further.

"Fuck, Ivy," he barks and places his hand behind my head.

My pussy is so wet that it's dripping into a puddle underneath me. I brace my hands against Evrin's large thighs as he eases himself into me.

I gag expectantly, but that only seems to turn him on further. Evrin gives me little time for a reprieve before he continues to slowly fuck my mouth.

"You have no idea how badly I've wanted this," he cries, "how desperately I've wanted to fuck this throat." He reaches down and wraps his hand around my neck just so he can feel his cock throat-fuck me.

I can't respond. I can only continue to take him as his strokes become harder and faster. Every gag is met with more cock. Every moan is met with a tight squeeze of my neck. I am powerless in this situation and couldn't be more turned on.

"Oh fuck, Ivy." Suddenly, his balls tighten, and his

shaft begins to throb. This is it, I'm finally going to make Evrin come. A sense of pride fills my chest.

He balls my hair in his fingers and suddenly thrusts his hips into my face. Before I know it, cum bursts into the back of my throat. The sensation is overpowering; whatever I expected, it wasn't this.

His seed forces its way down my throat, and I feel like I'm drowning. I try to push away upon instinct, but Evrin holds me in place.

"Take it. Fucking take it all, Ivy. You wanted me to claim your mouth. Well, now it's mine," he growls.

My sense of panic causes me to choke on his never-ending sperm and suddenly it starts spewing from my nose.

"Relax your throat, little dragonfly," Evrin coos and caresses the back of my neck with his thumb, "Come on, you can do it."

His voice relaxes me, and my brief moment of panic is soothed, knowing I'm in his arms. Before I know it, I'm sucking down his seed. It's fucking delicious.

Anything that doesn't fit down my throat right away slips out of my lips and drips down my body. By the time he finishes, I'm both filled and covered with Evrin's cum.

He suddenly pulls out, and I collapse to the ground, gasping for air. Evrin drops to his knees as if to worship me. "That was fucking incredible," he cries.

I'm exhausted already, but my lust knows no bounds.

"My turn." His voice drops a few octaves, and before I know it, he is turning me onto my back and spreading my legs.

I lie there completely limp as he tends to my throbbing pussy.

"Ahhh!" I scream as he buries his tongue into me.

"You are so fucking wet for me," he growls and returns to my clit.

My chest heaves as he finds the perfect pace and teases all the right places. He uses his free hands and grips my doughy thighs. The combination of sensations is euphoric.

Then, for the first time ever, his fingers slide down the inside of my thigh and brushes over my taint.

"Evrin," I gasp.

"Shh, I have to test how tight this pretty little pussy is," he moans and slowly slides one fat finger inside of me. An involuntary moan escapes past my lips, and he takes my body's encouragement in stride. But I'm stubborn and won't have him control every part of this claiming.

I use my very last strength to grab my wedding present, the dagger Evrin specially made for me.

I grip the dragonfly handle and push it against the thick skin along his neck.

Evrin freezes beneath my touch. "What are you—" he begins, but I cut him off.

"Don't think I haven't noticed your particular fetish for my neck." I say breathlessly. "Tell me, is it an orc thing or is it an Evrin thing?"

He chuckles deeply, which sends another wave of ecstasy through my core. With his finger still inside me, I know he can feel my wetness increase.

"It is an orc thing. We like to"—he ponders his words—"mark what belongs to us."

"Ah, I see. Then so shall I," I declare, digging the point of the dagger in slightly deeper. His thick skin doesn't penetrate easily.

"Fuck, you are so godsdamn sexy, Ivy," he growls and suddenly starts pumping his finger in and out of me while circling my clit with his tongue.

I scream out and dig my dagger in even further. I'm so close to coming.

"That's it," he breathes and laps at my pussy some more, "mark me."

Between the resistance of his skin and his relentless fingering, I feel like I'm going to shatter into a million pieces.

"Fucking do it, Ivy," he growls, "make me yours."

His words undo something inside of me, until I

finally break. As I come, I use just enough force to break his skin.

Evrin howls, and I feel a puddle forming beneath my ass.

I'm coming, and he is coming alongside me. Our juices intermingle with each other until we are both a mess.

We lie there panting in silence before he musters the strength to say, "That was fucking incredible."

Evrin reaches up to touch his neck, where I broke the skin. He studies the blood on his fingers before rubbing it across my belly.

"You look so sexy covered in all of my fluid," he groans, and I know he means it. He loves gripping my large ass, and I know if I let him, he would spend hours exploring every inch of my body.

I rub the mark I made on my mate's neck. I may not be an orc, but I sure can mark like one. A sense of pride swells in my chest, knowing I left a lasting impression on his body.

"I don't like wasting my seed," he grumbles, looking down at himself.

"I think you still have plenty of cum," I chuckle.

"Still, the only place worth coming is inside of you." He leans down and kisses my nipple.

They grow hard once more in anticipation, not long

after the overwhelming hunger for each other's bodies has returned. I question how much longer I'll be able to sustain this pace. In this given moment it feels like we could be out here for weeks.

"These breasts are unreal," he sighs and fondles them.

"I'm glad you like them because they hurt my back," I giggle.

"I fucking love them." He runs his tongue across both of them and squeezes them together. "But if they hurt your back, I guess I'll just have to massage you frequently."

"Mhm," I moan; that sounds like a good deal to me.

Evrin plays with my tits more and more until we've both worked each other up for another round.

Soon his hand slides down all of my rolls and curves until he finds my pussy. But he doesn't stop. Instead, he continues down even further until he reaches my asshole.

I suck in a sharp inhale as his finger teases my entrance. Luckily all of my cum has provided plenty of lubrication.

"Fuck, Ivy. This hole is so fucking tight," he growls and sucks on my nipple. "What are we going to do? I couldn't possibly fit my cock in there as is."

"I-I don't know," I falter and bite my lip nervously.

Evrin ever so slightly slides in his finger to stretch me. I cry out in both pain and pleasure.

"No, I definitely can't fit my cock in there just yet. We are going to need to train it first," he states matter-of-factly, and I have no idea what he is thinking.

"Good thing, I want to fuck your cunt first," he growls and nibbles at my nipple.

"Fuck!" I scream at the sharp sensation. The slight pain distracts me while he sinks his finger even deeper into my ass.

"That's it, Ivy. Fuck, you are such an obedient bride." He kisses me proudly. He retracts his finger and rises to his feet. I feel the sudden loss of his presence deeply. My heart clenches; I hate being away from him, even if he stands so closely.

"Come back," I whine.

"Soon, my bride," he chuckles and I watch as he unsheathes a long sword from his back. He takes a few steps and impales the blade into the ground.

Turning to me, he states plainly, "When your pussy is thoroughly fucked we are going to break in your ass."

His words catch me off guard, and it takes me a few moments to realize what he means. He plans to lower me onto the handle of his sword in preparation for his cock. Just the thought has my asshole clenching and pussy sopping wet.

"Fuck, are you burning up?" he shouts. "I'm so godsdamn hot."

As am I, a symptom of the fruit, I imagine. I don't know where I find the strength, but I pull myself to my feet. Evrin is quickly by my side, attempting to stabilize me. But I grab his hand and head towards the clear water surrounding the small island.

I wriggle my toes in the silt beneath me, which feels odd with my black stockings. However, the crisp water feels incredible on my skin. Evrin clearly agrees, as a loud groan emanates from his chest as his skin hits the water.

"Does that feel good?" I ask.

"Not as good as your pussy is going to feel around my cock," he groans, and before I know it, he wraps his arms around my waist and props my feet on top of his thighs.

Resting against his chest, I hover slightly over his throbbing dick. I'm only a few inches away from being impaled.

Evrin digs his fingers into my waist to get a good grip before he lowers me down.

"Fuck, Evrin!" I scream as the head of his cock meets my entrance. "I don't know if you are going to fit."

"I will, my little dragonfly," he reassures me. "Just relax and open yourself up to me."

I close my eyes and try to do as he says. At first, we go

slowly and allow the slickness of his cock to assist the process. Suddenly, I feel pressure, and then...he starts stretching me open.

"Fuck!" I scream in pleasure.

"By the gods, Ivy. You feel perfect," he groans.

"More!" I pant. "Give me more!"

He pushes deeper until he meets my uterus. He has nearly stuffed me completely, and I'm only halfway down his shaft. Determined to take more, I push myself down even harder.

"Ivy, you don't have to take—"

His words are cut short after I slide down his cock *hard*.

"Fuck!" he screams.

His cock protrudes against my womb. I look down and see my stomach bulge outlining his rock-hard member from inside. The sight is so fucking hot.

"Fuck me!" I yell. "Fuck my tight pussy."

"Yeah?" he growls and starts sliding in and out of me with more aggression. "Like this?"

"Harder!" I scream.

While he crouches in the water and I balance on his thighs, he starts pounding into me. I watch his cock fill my belly with every stroke, and his balls start slapping against my wet folds.

The noise is sticky and wet as I scream in pleasure.

His pre-cum seeps out of my cunt, and I want to beg him to breed me.

"You want more?" he growls into my ear. "Huh?!"

"Yes! Give it to me!"

I feel his tusks rub against the inside of my neck, and I know what is about to happen. Evrin is going to mark me while he fucks me.

"You're mine, Ivy," he screams while his balls slap against me. "Do you understand me?"

"This." *slap* "Cunt." *slap* "Is." *slap*. "Mine."

Suddenly, I feel a sharp pain along my neck, and I flail. Evrin holds me in place while he licks the blood running out of my new wound. I shatter under his touch. My vision goes hazy as I cry out. My orgasm wrecks my entire body, so he pauses his thrusts.

"Mine to *play* with, mine to *fuck*, and mine to *breed*," he whispers in my ear as I desperately try to catch my breath.

I slump against him, and he holds me, never pulling out. Once my breathing returns to normal, he decides it's time to leave the water. He turns me around so my legs wrap around his waist and carries me out of the cold water embrace.

Within a few strides, we are hovering over his sword. I'm nervous, horny, and desperate for him inside of me once more.

"Are you ready for me to train your ass?" he says matter-of-factly.

I simply nod my head. I'll do anything to feel him inside of me again.

He lowers me down to feel the sword handle with my pussy; the cylinder shape slides in between my folds, making sure to tease my clit.

"First, I'm going to wet this handle with your cunt, little dragonfly. Okay?" He checks in with me.

"Okay." I have complete trust in him.

He slides me down over the sword handle, and I take it easily. It's only half the size of his cock.

"Mmm, did you get it nice and wet?" he asks.

"Mhm," I moan.

He slides me off and makes sure that it's nice and slick. Once he knows it's ready for me, he shifts, and suddenly, it's at the entrance of my asshole.

"This is going to hurt, but I promise we will go slow," he says. "If you need me to stop, I'll stop."

"Okay," I whisper.

"The more you take, the lower you'll go," he explains. "Once you take enough, I'll make sure to breed your little human pussy."

"Fuck yes," I moan in response to his words. Not only will his sword be up my ass, but he plans on fucking my cunt in the process. The mere thought of the double penetration is turning me on like crazy.

Evrin lowers me down slightly, and I clench my jaw as the sword handle threatens to rip me open.

"Are you okay?" He pulls me in tighter to his chest.

"Keep going," I reassure him.

He does, and I scream out in pain as the handle's slickness slides inside of me, creating a ring of fire. My fingernails dig into his chest, and I cry out, but I don't want to stop.

Evrin pauses to let me adjust, and he continues only once I settle.

"That's it," he drawls, "let my sword handle stretch your tight little hole."

Before I know it, the excruciating pain starts turning into pleasure.

"Ivy, you've taken so much," he says, pulling back to look at me staked on his sword.

"It's starting to feel good." I bite my lip.

"Fuck, little dragonfly, I'm so desperate to be inside of you," he whimpers.

That's all the encouragement I need to take even more until I'm finally low enough to where his cock can enter my pussy.

"Do it," I scream. "Breed me, Evrin."

I'm not prepared for the sudden impact of his cock.

He slides in perfectly, but the pressure on both him and the sword is overwhelming.

"Say it again!" he screams.

"That I want you to breed me?"

"Fuck, yes! Say it! Fucking scream it until the whole godsdamn swamp can hear you." He barks out every word. I've never seen him this crazed.

"Fill up my cunt, Evrin! Flood my womb with your seed while your sword stretches my ass!" I shout at the top of my lungs.

Evrin roars with all of his might, and I suddenly feel hot spurts of cum shooting against my uterus. The sensation of my asshole being stretched and my cunt being full sends me over the edge.

My legs tremble, and I grip Evrins thick biceps for dear life.

He remains inside of me, and I know the second he pulls out, copious amounts of his white fluid will seep out.

"Just a few more seconds. I want to take every precaution to make sure you become pregnant."

I giggle quite pathetically against his sweaty chest.

"I'm sure there will be plenty of times to get me with child," I say, trying to catch my breath.

"And I will try valiantly each and every time," he

growls out his promise. Both my heart and pussy are full.

"Are you okay?" he whispers and kisses his mark on my neck

"More than okay," I reassure him. "That felt amazing."

"Good," I feel him smile against my skin, "because I still have to breed that fat ass of yours."

I clench involuntarily in response to his words.

"Only then will you be wholly and completely mine," he grumbles. "I will have claimed you, and nobody will ever be able to take you away from me."

His words hit me deeply. From this moment on I never want to be separated from him.

"Then do it." I kiss him gently. "Make me your wife. Make me your *mate*."

My words are enough to spur him into action as he slowly lifts me from his sword's handle. I grind my teeth at the discomfort, but it is no longer painful. However, Evrin's cock is bigger. So, I anticipate the pain will return to me shortly.

Evrin returns me to luscious mossy ground, but this time he turns me onto my hands and knees.

"You are fucking perfect," he declares, as he looks at my backside. "Do you know that? So godsdamn perfect."

His praises soothe my aches and strengthen my resolve.

"You might not be able to take all of me, and that's okay. But I need to fill this hole with my seed."

"Okay," I whimper, and he places his cock's head at my sore entrance.

I take in a sharp inhale as he presses forward slightly. "Oh fuck, this is tight," he groans.

He pushes a little harder, and I yelp, "Ow!"

"Do you need me to stop?" he asks. Always ensuring my safety.

"No, keep going. I'll tell you if I need to stop."

I feel his mushroom-shaped head sink into my hole, and I scream. It's both incredible and painful. His girth is so much bigger than the sword, I don't think I can take any more.

"Okay, stop. I think that's all I can take," I say with a shaky breath.

"Alright," he coos and caresses my back. The gentle touch feels so good and reassuring.

"We will have to train your ass on my swords every day to get you to take all of my cock," he explains as he spreads open my cheeks

"Mhm," I moan.

"I'll have to start making some new swords with

different handle thicknesses." He studies my hole and gently starts fucking me.

"Oh fuck, Evrin," I cry. "That feels so good."

"You are so tight, little dragonfly," he growls. "I can't take this anymore. I'm going to fucking explode."

I scream as he makes quick, short thrusts inside of me until the familiar sensation of a hot load explodes inside of me.

Evrin screams out in pleasure, and I moan as his seed soaks the inside of my walls.

We are both left panting as he quickly pulls out, and we collapse to the ground.

"Are you sure you are okay?" he asks worriedly. "You promise I didn't hurt you?"

"I promise." I smile. "I'm more than okay. That was...I don't have the words."

"Soul changing," he breathes and looks so deeply into my eyes that I feel like I could cry. This is all I've ever wanted.

"I love you, husband," I whisper.

"And I love you..." Evrin brushes a kiss across my cheek. "Wife."

8

EVRIN

"How long has the scout been gone?" Ivy shifts on her feet nervously. We arrived on the outskirts of our clan's village just after the sun reached its peak. In typical fashion, we were first greeted by a scout. With a newly claimed mate, I was ready to rip him to shreds when he first pointed his arrow at us.

However, it was Ivy who cooled down the situation. Now, we're waiting to be greeted by village elders and, hopefully, my family.

Ivy gasps, and I stand in front of her out of instinct. I'm horny, tired, and mad at anyone that looks at her. I spent the entire night rutting her, and I have no plans to stop when we arrive at our new home. Adjusting to clan life should be very interesting. Hopefully, we will settle into a new cabin and not see anyone for days.

"What is it?" I growl.

"Look!" she whispers and points at the horizon. "Is that them?"

Sure enough, a familiar green creature emerges with similar yet older features of my own.

"Mother," I whisper.

"Evrin?" My mother's voice cracks as she takes in the sight of me, I must look older, bigger even. Years living as an outcast will do that to an orc. But as my mother attempts to regain her emotions, my sister comes barreling forward.

"Evrin!" Celia screams and nearly knocks me over as she embraces me laughing. "How I've missed you, little brother!"

"I've missed you too." I smile. "Celia, this is Ivy, my mate, and Ivy, this is Celia, my sister."

"Hi," Ivy whispers. I've never seen or heard her act so shy. "Your brother has told me a lot about you. Pig stories and all."

Celia breaks into laughter. "Did he? Did he also tell you how I beat him up?"

"He did." Ivy shares a gentle smile.

I break my sister's embrace and wrap my hands around Ivy's waist to reassure her that I'm there.

My sister grabs her away from me and nearly strangles her in a hug. "It's so nice to meet you!"

I growl instinctively at my sister's aggressiveness towards my mate.

"Oh hush, she is fine," Celia scolds me. "I'm glad to see you are still just as moody as when you left."

That earns a chuckle from Ivy. Why do I feel they are already creating a secret alliance with each other?

I squint my eyes accusingly at my sister, but before we can quibble, my mother reaches us.

"Evrin! I knew you would return to us!" She beams. "You are too handsome to stay isolated."

Both Ivy and Celia snicker to each other.

"Mother..." I clear my throat. How is it that my family has already embarrassed me within the first few minutes of our reunion?

"And you—" She turns and faces Ivy. "Thank you for bringing back my son!"

They have a heartfelt moment, and I take in the sight of my family doting on my new mate. Ivy gives me a look of relief at their acceptance, and my heart swells. She deserves every ounce of happiness.

"Come, you two," my mother ushers, "the elders want to see you."

"Where are they?" I ask. "Shouldn't they be meeting us out here?"

"Zalk business, they've been discussing trade treaties for days," she brushes off the topic. "They expect you in the village square so Izel can inspect your new wife. After Kal brought home Riva and they had twin girls, she will be thrilled to hear you've returned home with another human." She smiles and brushes Ivy's hair out of her face. "Let's get you fed and cleaned up."

My sister slaps me on my shoulder. "It looks like Mother has a new favorite."

So it would seem," I laugh. "Where is your mate, Olgk, and the kits?"

"They are at home eagerly awaiting your return," Celia says.

"We can't wait." My heart constricts. It will be the first time I will meet my nephews.

Suddenly, more movement appears on the horizon. I immediately reach for Ivy's side, and my sister and mother also assume a battle stance. My heart swells at Ivy's acceptance into my family. They are clearly just as protective of her as I am.

The movement reveals itself to be yet another orc. But this time, the green flesh is accompanied by creamy pale skin. Kal and his mate, along with their two kits.

Kal holds on to a kit that is green with tusks, but she is slender with brown hair. Interestingly, her twin in her mother's arms looks exactly like her, perhaps a bit more timid.

Kal's mate hands over their daughter to him, and I can hear his growl, although I can't make out what he says. I'm shocked as the small female with golden hair starts walking towards us.

Kal eyes me down, as if to promise death should anything be happy to her. I know the feeling all too well. I give him a nod of reassurance. There is no animosity here—in fact, quite the opposite.

Ivy pushes me aside and runs out to meet her fellow human companion. There are a few moments of silence between the two before Ivy reaches out her hand. I quirk my eyebrow upwards as I study the greeting. Kal's mate takes her hand, and they shake.

"I'm Ivy," my mate says, smiling. "It's so good to meet you."

"Hi, Ivy. I'm Riva," she reciprocates the salutation with a grin of her own. "Shall I show you around?"

"I would love that!" Ivy beams. My mate pauses to look back at me and extends her hand for all of us to follow.

"She is going to do well here, brother," Celia teases.

"Oh, leave your brother alone, Celia," my mother scolds her. I can't help but laugh. Our relationship hasn't changed one bit since I've been gone.

"I hope so," I breathe.

"She will, son," my mother reassured me. "Just look at her, making friends already."

My lips upturn as I observe my mate talking enthusiastically with Riva. Ivy catches me staring and gives me an exasperated look. "Well come on!" she groans impatiently. "I want to see my new home."

"As you wish, my little dragonfly."

EPILOGUE: IVY

"You are a lifesaver, Ivy," Riva sighs while wrestling Elwen, one of her twin girls, to apply more of my swamp berry ointment to her gums.

"They are so much stronger than human babies!" she blurts, and I can't help but laugh.

Riva has it harder than most since she had twins eight months ago. Human twins are a handful, but kits? They are nearly impossible. They develop much quicker: walking, babbling, and developing unnatural strength by seven months old. Since Gwenna and Elwen are half-human, there are some minor differences between them and other orc kits their age. For starters, they have brown hair instead of the typical orc black. They also appear to be more lean, although they will most definitely get their father's height.

Luckily, Izel assured Evrin and me that I was only carrying one. A girl of my own. I place a hand over my stomach instinctively. It will still be a few months until she arrives. It didn't take long before I was pregnant, which wasn't much of a surprise. Evrin and I did little else other than fuck for the first weeks we were home.

"Elwen, hold still. This will help your tusks," Riva begs her little one, but it's Gwenna who soon comes barreling in to save her sister.

Growling, Gwenna grabs her mother and babbles something incoherent. It's funny observing the girls' dynamic. Gwenna is strong and outspoken, while Elwen is more shy and relies on her sister. But above anything else, their bond is unbreakable, even at such a young age.

"You tell her, Gwenna," I egg on.

"Not helping," Riva scolds me, and I laugh. The twins have been teething, making them more difficult than normal. Turns out their tusks breaking through their gums is very tedious business. Luckily, I perfected a little concoction out of swamp berries that helps alleviate some of their discomfort.

"Aha!" Riva yells. "Got it!"

Elwen makes a brief grunt in anger but decides she likes the sweetness.

"See, that wasn't so difficult, was it?" Riva enjoys her mini-victory.

The twins babble to each other in a language only they seem to understand before sitting down and playing with some of their toys.

Riva sighs in relief. "Maybe this time I'll get to sit for more than a few minutes."

"Don't worry, I'll take over," I assure her.

"Ivy, no, you don't have to. They are my—" she starts, but I cut her off.

"Hey! That's what friends are for. Besides, I need the practice."

"Gods, I love you. Every day, I'm so thankful Evrin found you," she muses.

"Stole me," I chuckle. "Minor difference but grateful nonetheless."

I stand and walk over to Riva's cabin window to overlook the village. This part of the swamp isn't nearly as wet as the rest. There are solid bits of ground with a busy town life, although the cabins are still built in the trees to save space.

"When do you think Evrin and Kal will be back?" she asks and takes a seat in the rocking chair next to me.

"Funny you ask..." I muse and point out the window to Evrin and Kal walking through town laughing. I smile, excited to see my big strapping orc. Normally, I help him craft his swords, but we worry the fumes aren't good for the baby since I'm pregnant. So now I spend most of my days with Riva. Not that I'm complaining. She has become my best friend ever since she introduced herself that very first day. She is my rock in this ever-changing world.

I smile to myself, I didn't think this life would be possible for me. All those years I spent alone banished from my own people. Scared of the very creatures who soon welcomed me in as one of their own. No longer am I haunted by the man who I once thought stole everything. But he can't steal this. I rhythmically rub my stomach, and admire my mate.

Riva stands to see out the window for herself, and we smile at each other. I know she missed Kal just as much as I missed Evrin.

Suddenly, a bird ascends from the sky, capturing Evrin and Kal's attention. Their smiles turn serious.

"What is it?" I look nervously at Riva for an explanation.

"It's Sylas," she whispers and shakes her head, realizing I have no idea who that is. "He is one of the clan's hunters. He lives far north and only drops his contributions to the clan once a season."

"Is that why we must wait so long for the good hide to return to the markets?" I ask.

"Yeah." She nods. "He may be the least frequent hunter, but he is definitely the best. Kal says he pays equal contributions as everyone else but delivers it in larger batches to save on trips."

"So what's with the bird?"

"It's how he communicates with clan leaders. No one has seen him in years. Not even the scouts. All we know is that he lives at the farthest part of the swamps, near the base of the mountain. He only sends messages via carrier pigeons when something has happened."

"The mountain?" My eyes widen. "As in *thee* mountain?"

Since I arrived, the tension with the Zalk has only grown. Their new leader, Grul, is a fanatic obsessed with growing a warrior clan.

"Mhm." She nods her head. "Something must have happened! The last message we got was right before you and Evrin arrived."

"But why is he so far north? Surely, he would have better chances of finding a mate if he was closer to the clan."

"Well, that's just it; he doesn't want a mate," she shouts exasperatingly.

"What?" I shake my head, not understanding. "No way."

"Yes, way!" She nods. "Kal told me the whole story."

"Fascinating," I muse out loud. Kal is a reliable source and a blabbermouth.

"That's not even half of it." She turns and drops her voice an octave. That's her gossip voice. Oh, this is going to be good.

"You can't tell anyone that I told you this. Kal will kill me," she makes me promise.

"I swear." I hold my right hand up, knowing that I'm going to share with Evrin. But Riva knows that.

"Sylas has already been to the Chosen One," she whispers.

"No!" I gasp. "With who?"

"Aeryn."

"The baker's mate?!" I can't believe what I'm hearing.

"Yup. It turns out Sylas and her have been friends since they were kits. They assumed they were mates, but when they went to the Chosen One, the fruit, well, it had the opposite intended effect."

"We will be either ignited with passion *or* fueled with animosity," I repeat the word Evrin recited to me before our ceremony. A chill runs down my spine at the thought.

"Exactly. Ever since then, he has sequestered himself away up north." Her voice has a tinge of sadness.

"Why haven't I heard this story before?" I ask.

"The clan likes to keep it under wraps. The only

reason Kal knew was because he helped break them up when they went for each other's throats."

"Shit," I groan. That must have been awful.

Suddenly, a commotion breaks out in the square. Green bodies start gathering around, shouting questions.

"What the—?" Riva asks, but I grab her arm and pull her to the door. "I'll grab Gwenna, and you grab Elwen. Let's go check out what's going on. I'm too nosey to just sit and watch. Besides, our mates are down there."

"Good idea," she agrees, and we each grab a kit.

While we usher ourselves down the stairs and towards the crowd, Evrin pops out from the sea of people. He catches a glimpse of me and then Riva.

"Kal!" she shouts and nods his head over to the male's respective mate.

"You two should get back to the cabin, little dragonfly." He rushes over to me. Kal isn't far behind and takes Gwenna from my arms.

"What, why? What's going on?" I ask, confused.

"Kal?" Rivas's voice is laced with concern. Her mate bends down and kisses her on the forehead for reassurance.

"The elders just got a message from Sylas," Kal says.

"That's a hunter in the north," Evrin tries to fill me in.

"Riva explained who he is already," I assure him.

"What did the message say?" Riva asks.

Kal and Evrin glance at each other worriedly before Evrin finally responds, "A Zalk soldier stole a human from one of the towns up north and dragged her into the swamp."

Both Riva and I gasp.

"According to Sylas, he was attempting to kill her before he intervened," he continues.

"Intervened how?" I ask.

"Sylas shot and killed him," Kal states matter-of-factly.

"Surely that's self-defense. The orc was attempting to murder an innocent," Riva rationalizes.

"Yes, but the Zalk might not see it like that," Evrin grumbles. "Grul will find any excuse to put his warrior orc clan to use." I haven't seen my mate like this. He and Kal both look incredibly worried.

"So what now"? I ask hesitantly.

"Pray to the gods that we didn't just enter a war with the Zalk," Kal sighs.

So that's what I do, I pray. Pray for my unborn baby, for our clan, and for that poor female who was taken.

NEXT IN THE SERIES

JOIN MY PATREON

Interested in seeing NSFW art? Scan QR code below

ALSO BY K.L. WYATT

Brides of the Frostwolf Clan Series

Stolen by the Orc Commander: An Enemies to Lovers Monster Romance

Start reading here

A human girl set on revenge...

Orcs and humans have been at war with each other for as long as Snow can remember. Orphaned as a child, she has spent her years as a tracker, known only as the 'Hooded Bandit' by the king's men. Stealing anything she can in order to survive the harsh human lands of Everdean. The only thing keeping her going is the determination to make those responsible for her family's death suffer.

When a routine carriage robbery goes south, Snow finds herself face to face with the notorious orc commander himself. Taken as his captive and returned to Orc Mountain, Snow has a new goal: escape from the mountain no matter the cost.

An orc commander determined to end the war...

Azogg the Destroyer is a skilled fighter. As leader of the orc army, he despises humans more than most. The war has destroyed their homelands, leaving them all to suffer in the mountains. As commander, he knows that he must find a way to end this conflict once and for all.

With no other choice, Azogg finds himself tracking a royal advisor...only to have his plans upended by a sickly human female. One he quickly discovers is not what she seems. Azogg is resistant to trusting a human, but her extensive knowledge of the royal trade routes makes her the ultimate find.

Could this human be the key to ending the war?

Tempers and passion flare as both Snow and Azogg realize the only way forward is for them to work together. Will this unlikely pair be able to put aside decades of hate and distrust? Or will factors beyond their control drive them apart before they get the chance?

Welcome to Orc Mountain.

My Orc Valentine: A Brides of the Frostwolf Clan Novella
Book 1.5

Also by K.L. Wyatt

Start Reading <u>here</u>

The orcs and humans have recently formed a tentative allyship, ending the decades long feud they have been locked in. Now, the two species are trying to navigate coexisting within their new world.

On the night of Lupercalia, a festival celebrating love, Lyra is shocked to see a group of orc soldiers arrive at the human brothel she works at. However, she can't afford to worry about the one who keeps casting curious looks her way. Lyra is freshly eighteen and in the spirit of the holiday her mistress has decided she would make the ultimate prize by auctioning off her virginity to the highest bidder. She is shocked when the male she caught staring at her earlier seems the most intent on winning her. The young orc soldier named Zhor soon out bids the others; his eyes promising a night of passion that Lyra won't ever forget.

As apprehension gives way to unbridled passion, Lyra grapples with the fact that the feelings growing between her and Zhor can only last the night. Even if she finds herself wishing Lupercalia never ends.

Chained to Krampus: A Holiday Novella

Start Reading <u>here</u>

With the Christmas season fast approaching, a decades-long tradition looms closer. A tradition that is as macabre as it is longstanding. For every seventy years, the townspeople must choose who amongst them is to be sacrificed to Krampus.

At twenty-seven years old, Holly is still a virgin and

determined to keep it that way. However, her life takes an unexpected turn when she rejects the town's mayor and is chosen as Krampus's sacrifice. Expecting to die at the hands of this cruel beast, Holly is shocked to learn that her new captor has different intentions in mind. Ones that will bind them together forever and leave her round with his child. Desperate for her freedom, she finds herself chained to the horrific creature as he seeks to claim more than just her body.

Despite his monstrous nature, Holly soon learns there is more to this Krampus than meets the eye.

Kristof, the only living Krampus, has lived alone for many years. Bound by his duty to continue his kind's lineage, he eagerly awaits the arrival of his human offering. When he meets his virgin sacrifice, she is nothing short of perfection. The only issue is that her feelings are not reciprocated. In fact, she recoils at his mere presence. When Holly tries to flee, he has no choice but to shackle her to him. Will Kristof be able to show his new mate that they are more similar than she thinks? Or will the chains that bind them only serve to drive them further apart?

ABOUT THE AUTHOR

Kayla, is a smut obsessed 20-something year old, that didn't discover her love for books until later in life. Her new hobby soon became an obsession she wished to share with others and thus her Booktok account was created. Little did she know that this would change the trajectory of her life forever.

Now, two and half years later she has a new ambition, becoming a romance author. She loves all things monsters, but especially Orcs. Combining her beasts with fantasy, she hopes all of her readers have monster-loving time with her new series, Brides of the Frostwolf Clan.

Originally from the Midwest, Kayla works from home in her small Connecticut apartment with her boyfriend and two cats. When she isn't engrossed in her latest read, she is conducting Tarot readings for her friends, watching Love Island, and playing the Sims.

Keep up to date by signing up to my newsletter!

Made in United States
Troutdale, OR
06/29/2024